I0819672

HUNGERED

HUNGERED

A NOVEL

AMANDA RIZKALLA

HENRY HOLT AND COMPANY
NEW YORK

Henry Holt and Company
Publishers since 1866
120 Broadway
New York, New York 10271
www.henryholt.com

EU Representative: Macmillan Publishers Ireland Ltd.,
1st Floor, The Liffey Trust Centre,
117–126 Sheriff Street Upper, Dublin 1, D01 YC43

Distributed in Canada by Raincoast Book Distribution Limited

Library of Congress Cataloging-in-Publication Data

Names: Rizkalla, Amanda, author.
Title: Hungered : a novel / Amanda Rizkalla.
Description: First edition. | New York : Henry Holt and Company, 2026.
Identifiers: LCCN 2025048709 | ISBN 9781250420756 (hardcover) |
ISBN 9781250420763 (ebook)
Subjects: LCGFT: Fiction | Novels
Classification: LCC PS3618.I9346 H86 2026
LC record available at https://lccn.loc.gov/2025048709

First Edition 2026

Designed by Kelly S. Too

Printed in the United States of America

10 9 8 7 6 5 4 3 2 1

For Abuela

Some things can't be said inside houses.

—Irene Solà, *When I Sing, Mountains Dance*, translated by Mara Faye Lethem

HUNGERED

Mama says we eat with our eyes.

"Te vas a ahogar," she says, that I will choke if I look too long. Lava cakes spilling out the center, quesadillas with bell peppers grilled flat inside—Third Street has everything our eyes could want. Our eyelids are teeth that close shut. Each blink, a bite, she says.

We go window-shopping, the three of us. We hold hands and point and tell each other to look. Look at all of these people and their four-dollars-per-macaron. Look at us and the four-dollar shirt my brother is wearing, plus tax, so four forty, and that is almost twenty minutes of mama at work, this shirt.

"I want the rainbow kind," Rafa says, pointing to an ice cream shop a block ahead. This time he cries, he wants it so bad. I want it too—a scoop of vanilla. Chocolate sprinkles. Then mama does what she always does, says what she always says.

"Mijo." She cups his cheek in her palm. "We eat with our eyes."

When we get back to the car, mama unlocks the trunk and tosses her purse inside. It lands in a thud next to the trash bags she stuffed with our clothes last week, when we got in the car and drove for an hour before Rafa asked why we were running away. Mama says that we were not using our feet, so we were not running away, just driving.

"Can't we get a hotel room?" I ask, closing the trunk.

She breathes out, looks at my face, brown eyes to brown eyes. She runs a thumb across the soft of my cheek.

"We're fine," she says. Then she whispers it. She tells me to get in the car.

Eleven p.m., the dashboard blinks at us. Seventy-four degrees outside, tank half full, and why are we here? After mama takes out the keys and the low, steady rumble of the engine sighs into silence, she looks at us in the rearview mirror and says it is time for bed, the night a starry black curtain pulled tight across our windows. And then mama is snoring a few minutes later, a rumble of her own, her head heavy on the pillow she has propped on the steering wheel. My brother falls asleep on my shoulder. Careful not to wake him, I reach for my jacket in the seatback pocket, unzip it, and spread it across our chests.

When mama and I wake in the morning, I lift Rafa's head from my shoulder and rest it on a bundle of clothes—the yellow sweater I wore the day before, the puffy olive jacket teta mailed in a padded envelope from Egypt for my birthday last month. I climb into the passenger seat. We watch the sunrise together, mama and me. We watch it from the window. The sun has caught on the hook, the fisherman has reeled it up, and it sits flat and bright against the blue, dying.

"Mama," I try again. "What about school?"

She says nothing.

The next day:

"Mama?"

"Sofia," she says. "Stop."

We go to the public library, where the soap in the bathroom pumps out in pearly white droplets. I hold them in my hands for a moment, the shimmering, slippery beads, and wonder who I could trick. If I could sun-bake them into pearls and sell them. Then maybe we could sleep on real beds tonight. We wash our faces, our necks, holding each other's hair back from behind. Mama passes me the toothpaste from inside her bag, and I squeeze a peppermint trail onto my index finger. I swish warm water around inside my mouth—swishing, swishing—then spit it out. Rafa does the same. We rub toothpaste around our gums, our teeth, reaching in deep, and swish that, too. Mama washes underneath her arms and pats herself dry with a clump of brown paper towels. "All clean?" she asks.

"All clean," we say.

When we drive to tonight's parking lot, mama makes sure to stop at all of the stop signs because Camila, her friend from nursing school, told her that one time, around here, a police officer stopped one of her cousins for running a red light and then asked for his driver's license. It all went downhill from there, she said. He is gone now.

"But anyway," Camila said, walking into her kitchen to refill the water pitcher. It was a few days before we left baba and we were over at her house for dinner. "I'm sure Rhonda will put in a good word for you at the clinic," she said, the knob squeaking as she turned on the faucet. "Plus, they're short-staffed. They need people."

Mama sighed. "I really hope so."

"And your nursing license?"

Mama smoothed out a frayed corner of the place mat. She said she had kept it active, renewing it every two years ever since she stopped working seven years ago, when she had Rafa. If she let her license expire, it would become "delinquent," and she did not like the way that sounded. "It's renewed through next year."

Camila nodded. "Then you're all set." She poured water into our glasses, the spout poking out like a beak from the pitcher.

We had tilapia for dinner that night, with crunchy battered-over fins, bones as thin as sewing needles, eyes like plump, clouded marbles. Camila made one for each of us, stuffing their bellies full of lemon slices and rosemary and garlic before dredging them in flour and deep-frying them. She kept a bowl of candy on a bench by the front door, left over from Halloween the week before. She offered some to us before we left her house, shaking the candy until it rattled in the bowl, the gold chocolate coins, lollipops the color and cut of jewels—ruby, amethyst, topaz. I wish I had taken some.

We are parked outside of the market when Rafa asks mama for a bedtime story.

"A real-life one," he says.

"Okay, let me think," she says, groaning as she readjusts herself in her seat. It surprises me every time how loud it is when her elbows pop. Mama calls herself an old lady even though thirty-six does not seem old to me, but her knees and neck and back say otherwise, cracking alive when she moves, buckling into place. I stretch my right elbow into a straight line, doing the math in my head. Twelve is a third of the way to thirty-six. No pop, though. Not yet.

"A real-life story," she says, tapping her finger on her chin. "Well, all I can say is don't trust men you meet at gas stations. Especially you, mija. Don't trust men at all."

Rafa and I look at each other.

"I should've just taken the car to the mechanic that day," she says. At this point, she knows we are listening. We do not talk about baba anymore, not really. This story, though, we already know by heart. About how, with a car engine as loud and roaring as her laugh, mama turned into the gas station near the champurrado stand. About how the car spurted como un pedo, then died, dead, in front of her. About how she asked the nice-looking stranger in a plaid shirt pumping gas next to her if he knew anything about cars.

"And he fixed it con ganas," she says, smiling into her words.

Then there was a first date, then a wedding date. Then there was me, then Rafa, and some bruja who made baba's heart gone.

"He's an asshole," she says, breaking her trance, rubbing her temples. "Pump your own gas, Sofia," she says to me. "Fix your own car." Solemn for a heartbeat, her eyes closed in thought. "Believe me."

Early the next morning, mama's phone buzzes in the cup holder, angry as a cicada. "Wait here," she says, stepping out of the car and closing the door before she answers her phone, her footsteps trailing off in the gravel.

"Where would we go?"

Rafa giggles.

It is just becoming morning, and the sun is gray-white, moon-like. It is gloomy and smells like earthworms, like wet dirt, and I want to ask mama if it is going to rain. She says she knows in her bones when it will happen, that they ache right before the sky starts to spill. Rafa and I watch as she kicks up asphalt with her shoes.

When she comes back inside, she is smiling. "They're letting me start on Monday," she says, putting her phone back into the cup holder. Mama says this is a reason for us to celebrate. She opens the center storage compartment, reaches her hand under a layer of napkins—some brown, some white, some imprinted with restaurant logos—and pulls out three red candies, handing one to me and one to Rafa and keeping one for herself. They are stop-sign-red, wrapped in clear plastic with green-light-green polka dots. I twist the wrapper off mine.

"Candy for breakfast?" Rafa asks, perking up.

"Better than nothing," I say.

I put it in my mouth. Sour cherry. My jaw aches, sore from the sourness, and the feeling reminds me of a few days ago, when my stomach felt like that, when mama looked at the way I was folded over myself, clutching my stomach because I was so hungry, and asked if I had cramps, if I started my period. I shook my head. We drove to a bank, and she told me to go check in the bathroom, handing me a small wad of napkins in case there was blood. There was not. "I'm just hungry," I said when I got back into the car. I tried to sleep it off, but the air was so hot, so thick, everything felt like it was happening in slow motion, moving my hand across my chest to put on my seat belt, rolling the windows down for air. I place the wrapper on my lap.

"We had these the whole time?" I ask.

Mama nods, crumpling her wrapper into a small ball. "I was saving them for something good."

I turn away from her, looking out the window. It starts to rain.

She says that yesterday we drove west and today we are driving north, and that, fingers crossed, we will have enough gas to keep driving until we reach the clinic. This was not the clinic she had planned to work at—the one where she had worked with Camila for five years, where she knew every doctor and nurse and receptionist by name, every night-shift janitor—but mama shrugs and says, "We'll see how it goes."

I lean my head against the seat belt strap. We drive past bare trees, their red leaves shed like clothing at their feet. The puddles reflect the sky, each one a round, flat mirror on the sidewalk. The windshield wipers squeak with each swipe, sending sprays of water off the sides.

When mama stops at a red light, I reach forward from the back seat to tap her elbow. Up close she smells like her perfume, jasmine and honey, like a strongly brewed tea, a tea bag steeped in a mug a little too long. "How far away are we?"

"From the clinic? Maybe another thirty minutes or so."

"No," I say. "From home."

"A few hours," she says quietly, her eyes on the road. "Maybe three."

"Only three?" We have been driving for days. "Have we been going in circles?"

I never liked cleaning my room. At home, I would let dust coat my windows like dryer lint before finally listening to mama and taking a wet paper towel to the glass. My clothes, a mountain range of frilly skirts, dark jeans, and long-sleeve dresses on my bedroom floor. Baba said we must—and that was the word he used, "must"—keep the house clean. He worked his whole life for this house, he would say, then tell us, again, how he got here, that he moved here all alone when he was in his twenties, with two hundred dollars and a brown suitcase and three words in English: "water," "church," and "Lemonbalm," the street where his cousin lived. He was proud of the house. "Four bedrooms, three bathrooms, a pool, and a hot tub," he would tell anyone who asked. The contracting company he hired did most of the work, but the paint, all the paint in the house, came from his own company. The violet in the dining room. The cloudy white of the kitchen cabinets. The teal ceiling in his office.

Today I sweep crumbs, gritty as sand, off the car seats and into my palm. I consider eating them but then notice a dead ant in the pile and toss it all out the door, the dried grains of rice, the bits of crackers and granola bars. The ant, curled like a comma in my palm. I reach into my backpack for the red hibiscus flower I picked from a bush earlier this morning and stick the stem into my seatback pocket, the flower bright as a flame against the gray seat.

Later, while Rafa plays with his toy cars, vrooming them over the headrests, honk-honking them, and while mama reads an old newspaper she found in the trunk, using her finger to follow along, mumbling to herself, I reach across them to pick up tissues, empty water bottles, dirty clothes. The way things pile up so quickly afterward, it is like they do not notice. While we are getting ready for bed, I wince at mama's newspaper splayed out on the passenger seat, unfolded. I check the front seats, then the back. There are toy cars in every cup holder.

"Could you please pick that up?" I ask Rafa, pointing to the plastic T. rex he dropped face down on the floor.

He shakes his head. "He's sleeping."

"I said please."

"Say pretty please."

"Pretty please."

"Say pretty-pretty-most-beautiful please," he says, crossing his arms.

I groan, throwing my head back.

Rafa smiles and picks up another dinosaur by its tail. A stegosaurus. He drops it and it lands on top of the T. rex. "What?" he says, looking up at me. "He was lonely."

Mama sits up and lays her pillow flat on its back, the mascara and lipstick stains on the cover like the abstract paintings I learned about in art class last year—red smudge here, black line there, mostly white canvas. If the car is a museum, I am looking at the other exhibits around me. Plastic Rice Bowl Under Seat,

Blue Scrubs Draped Over Headrest, Tissues Stuffed into Door Pocket, Dirty Socks in Plastic Bag.

Outside: Overfilled Fly-Buzzing Green Dumpster, Flattened Oil-Stained Pizza Box, White Napkins Covering Ground Like Snow.

When mama goes to work on Monday morning, we wait in the car with the windows rolled down. The air gusts inside, cooling off the car seats, the vinyl hot, steaming. It feels too hot, too humid, too sticky for the second week of November. Rafa starts to fidget around noon before mama is supposed to meet us for her lunch break. His stomach growls an angry growl, and mine a sad, low drone, and he declares himself the winner of empty stomachs. He wants a prize.

"Peanut butter cookies, please," he says.

"Coming right up," I say, and pretend to crack an egg into a bowl, mixing it with a plastic spoon I found under my seat. "Help me shape them into cookies?" He nods and cups the invisible dough into balls before flattening them into disks between his palms. When I take them out of the oven—a tissue box—I can almost smell them. Nutty and roasted and sweet.

Rafa pouts. "I want real ones."

"I know," I say. "Me too."

The heat in the car is like an aunt who does not stop smothering us. Even with the windows open all the way, the heat is hugging us, kissing us, pinching our cheeks. Its perfume—hot, hot vinyl—sharp in our noses. I try to read to Rafa, but my stomach-ache makes me dizzy, and the words lift off the page and flit around me like lazy bugs, the letters sprouting wings to fly off to better places. To keep him from crying, he and I play counting games and then the quiet game, waiting for mama. When we play I Spy, he tells me over and over again what he spies with his littlest eye, and it is always parking lot–related because we are parked here, behind the clinic. He spies lampposts, uniformed delivery men, and a folded-in-half parking ticket picked up by the wind, fluttering like a butterfly, free.

On her lunch break, mama walks us over to the library still wearing her scrubs. The library is a one-story brick building with two white pillars up front sticking out like tusks, smooth and thin. To the left of the revolving door, there are doily-shaped pink flowers, plants with leaves as big as elephant ears.

"Here," she says, reaching into her purse to hand an apple to Rafa and a pear to me, a handful of napkins to both of us. "From the break room." I bite into the pear, its juice so sweet I feel like I have bitten into a sack of perfume, pale yellow juice dripping down off the side of my mouth. I wipe it with the back of my hand.

"So, what do you say if someone wants to steal you?" she asks us with her hands on her hips. It is our ritual, her question, my answer.

"That my mom would pay them to."

Mama winks. "That's right."

When we finish, we toss the cores into the square mouth of the trash can. They reach the bottom in a thump. Mama pats Rafa's head then ruffles his hair. "Be good," she tells him, touching his cheek. "Listen to your sister."

From one to four, I find a book, a chair in the corner, and

watch the sun settle around me like an orange shawl as I turn the pages. At four thirty, pink streaks the sky, like the time mama stepped on the brakes too fast at an intersection and the tires scraped the road black.

I walk through the aisles, passing through physiology, philosophy, parenting. In the parenting section, I thumb through a thick manual titled *Adolescent Child-Rearing* and stop on a chapter titled "Methods of Reinforcement: Positive or Negative?" After skimming a few paragraphs, I decide that baba used negative reinforcement, that positive reinforcement makes more sense to me, and that I will practice on my brother.

Later that night, after mama sets herself up with her pillow, Rafa says his prayers like abuelo taught him when we last saw him, three years ago at abuela's funeral: *God, thank you for the car, for mama, for Sofia, for the peanut butter cookies today.*

Mama turns her head back to look at us. "Cookies?"

"Made-up cookies," I say.

"Oh," she says. "What's a made-up cookie?"

I open up the book I checked out. The index card tucked inside the book says my name, almost like it belongs to me. And it does for two weeks.

"Besitos," mama tells Rafa when he finishes his prayers. He makes his way to the front seat and gives her his forehead, which she stamps with a kiss, her vanilla lip balm leaving an oily gloss on his skin.

After a few minutes, I turn on the overhead light on my side. It yellows the first page. For a few minutes, until my eyes get heavy and the words blur, unfocused, I am a girl on a farm eating sun-warmed strawberries, real ones, plucking off the stems and leaves in one quick pull, as if I were removing a feathery green hat from the top of each one, balding them. She must choose between man one and man two. They have names, but I am so sleepy, I cannot remember them, and besides, there are strawberries to eat—strawberries so real they could probably stain her shirt red.

Mama drives us to a new market the next day. When we get there, I walk up to the lady with the red apron untied behind her back, the strings grazing the floor. I watch as she uses tongs to flip shrimp on the small grill and they pop and sizzle into white noise. She presses one into the grill with the flat edge of her tongs. It sputters garlic butter, steaming. My stomach rumbles. It smells like a restaurant.

I point at the Free Sample sign. "Can I have one?"

"Of course."

She puts one in a small cup, red tail arching over the side, and I reach to take it. "Is it okay if I take an extra one for my brother?"

"I don't see why not," she says.

She hands me another one.

Shrimp, butternut squash ravioli, pour-over coffee from Ethiopia. Handfuls of sample cups, extra coffee for mama, we bring them back to the car and set them down on the center divider. Mama takes out one of the instant rice bowls she bought, which she microwaved inside the store, and reaches inside the glove compartment for our three plastic spoons. She wipes each of them off with a napkin before handing them to us. We turn on the radio. She spins the knob, skipping back the stations, blips of static and mid-song belting and news coverage, until she finds the Spanish one, then turns it up loud.

"Oh, Sofia," she says, looking at me. "This was the song. *The* song. Even your abuelo knows the words." She divides the rice into three, taking the smallest third for herself. I set down my spoon. At the mention of abuelo, I can see it—the three of us on an air mattress in mama's old bedroom, abuelo stirring a large pot of champurrado on the stove, telling us to come, come quick before it gets cold.

We can stay with him.

The way mama is looking at me, it is like she knows what I am thinking. I open my mouth to speak.

She puts her hand up. "Don't."

"Don't what?"

She changes the subject. "So, what time did you go to sleep last night?" she asks.

"Maybe midnight. But, mama—"

"How is it so far?" she asks, motioning to the library book with her chin. I tucked my pencil inside the book last night, holding my spot at chapter three.

"Why does she get to stay up late?" Rafa asks.

"She's reading. Reading's good for you." Mama takes a sip of her coffee, blowing it first so it cools. I know even the briefest mention of abuelo is enough to simmer mama into a steady boil, but she brought him up first. We have not seen him since abuela's funeral, though I do not know why. I take a bite out of the ravioli—a food pocket, Rafa called it inside the market—and see the orange mush of the filling inside. I take another bite.

"I want to stay up late too," he says.

Mama sighs. "Do you want a book from the library?"

"If I get a book, then I can stay up late?"

"Only if you read it."

"Then no."

"Your choice, mijo," mama says, and then turns to face me. "What were you saying?"

I smooth over the cover with my hand. "Nothing." She could have paid attention if she wanted to.

"No," she says. "Tell me."

"Just that I like the book." I say it through my teeth.

"Oh," she says. "Good. That's good."

After we finish eating, mama tells us to put on our seat belts.

"Which way do you want to go?" she asks, and starts to pull out of the market parking lot, waiting for a man to cross in front of her with his shopping cart, the little girl on his shoulders covering his eyes. The girl throws her head back with laughter, and her two braids swing back too. The man is smiling, toothy, pushing his cart slowly, steadily, over the speed bump. There are apples and apples and apples in their grocery bags, I imagine. A gallon of milk. A carton of eggs. Sliced bread. The usual. All the things that people whose dads carry them like that, over their shoulders, would get at a market.

"Turn left," Rafa says, and I agree, "Left."

After the man finishes crossing, mama signals, and we turn.

"Do you remember me telling you about this street?" she asks. "I used to buy oranges with abuela here when I was *this* small," she says, bringing her index finger and thumb *this* close together. "Here at this corner, see?"

Rafa says he remembers. "Can we buy some?"

"No, honey. Next time."

He frowns. "That's what you always say."

When the light turns green, she pulls into a parking lot for an old church with overgrown vines sprawling the stained-glass windows, then turns the car off.

"There's a new market a few streets over," she says, twisting her keys out from the ignition. "We'll go there tomorrow."

The three of us tell each other what we wish we had. It is a game we play when none of us can sleep. We play it often.

"TV," mama says.

"Lena and Chloe," I say. My closest friends from school. "It's Chloe's birthday tomorrow."

"The couch."

"Strawberries."

My gaze shifts to Rafa, and I realize he has not offered one in a while. I nudge him from across the car. "You got one?"

His cheeks are red, his lips are chapped. Slowly, he meets my gaze. "Baba."

Mama is up late tonight filling out some forms for work, so the overhead light is on, a square yellow sun beaming down so bright I can still see it when I close my eyes. I finished my library book an hour ago and still cannot fall asleep. Counting sheep is not working even though mama says it works for her.

"Almost done?" I ask her.

"Almost."

I pull my jacket over my head, close my eyes, and try again, seeing the sheep, with wool dense like cauliflower, jump over a wooden fence. I imagine myself sleeping in my old bed, drowsy-eyed and comfortable under the weight of my quilt, my pillow near the window mama let me keep open in the summer. The girl might be sleeping there now, tucked into my sheets. I still do not know her name.

It was mid-October, two days after my birthday, when the girl began living in my bedroom. That day, we came home from school to see baba lugging a duffel bag into my room, dragging it across the hardwood floor by its handle. The metal zipper carved a thin white line into the wood. I saw the outline of a slim, pale nose before he closed the door. A flash of long black hair. He said Rafa and I would have to share a room from now on. Just that. No explanation.

"But, baba, my stuff," I said, thinking about my books, my gel pens, my watercolors, the turquoise seahorse Lena saw me admiring in a storefront window and bought with her own allowance for my birthday. They were all on my desk. If he would just let me grab them.

"Stop," he said, pressing his back against my bedroom door. "Later." His arms were crossed like a bodyguard's, a vein crawling up his forearm like a green worm.

Mama pretended not to see her. When the girl walked into the kitchen, taking a bag of potato chips from the cupboard before returning to my room, mama would look past her. Sometimes mama bumped into her, stumbling into the side of a table and saying Damn it or Cabrona but never Sorry. The first time

I saw her come out of my room, I looked at her belly, which looked as round and tight as a small watermelon, the fabric of her shirt—my tie-dyed shirt, I realized—stretching thin around her belly button.

"Isn't that mine?" I asked.

But she hurried back into my room before she could answer.

At night, when it was late and Rafa's breath would steady and I could tell he was asleep, I wondered what the slightest pinprick of one of mama's sewing needles would do, if air would burst out of her belly loudly like a whoopee cushion. If she would pop or disappear altogether. Then I could have my room back.

"Do you know who she is?" I asked Rafa one night before bed. I thought she might be one of baba's cousins visiting from Egypt, but I was not sure.

He did not answer.

I nudged him. "Rafa."

"What?"

"The girl. You know who she is?"

He turned over and faced me. "The bruja? No. Mama says if you make eye contact with a bruja, you'll turn into one." Then he groaned. "Sofia, you woke me up."

"Okay, okay, go back to sleep."

We turned away from each other, and again I heard his breath steady.

Tonight, a few minutes after mama turns off the overhead light, I hear it, the knocking, and my eyes flicker open, and there, at the window, is a man. It is dark out and I can close my eyes to make him gone, simple as that, but I hear it and cannot stop hearing it. Knock, knock. Knuckles on glass.

"Eyes down. You're asleep," mama says, whispering, and her lips barely move. "Look like it."

"Can—" I start.

"Sleep. He'll leave soon."

I want to ask her if she would honk the horn because it worked last time. But he just knocks and knocks and continues knocking. Then he speaks:

"Just wanted to know if you're looking to kick it or something. If you're looking to hang out. Shit, I'd pay. Only if you're good, though—you'd have to be good. I can see you, by the way. Three of you, at least, in there. You could be a baby sugar. Or, uh, no, that's not it. A sugar baby. Sorry, I'm buzzed. How old is the girl, by the way? Is she a woman yet?"

Mama clenches her jaw.

Am I a woman yet? I want to ask mama but she would tell me to sleep.

One night at home, I waited twenty whole minutes for Rafa to fall asleep. I wanted to ask the girl who she was, why she was here. I looked over at my brother, curled up on his side, holding a plastic dinosaur to his chest with his fingers wrapped around its torso. Drool dripped off the side of his mouth, pooling on his pillow like a small pond. I grabbed a tissue from the bed-side table and wiped it off. Then I slipped out of bed and walked down the hall, past the framed pictures of abuelo, abuela, teta, and giddo, looking down at the hardwood floor to avoid their eye contact.

My bedroom door was wide open. The window was open, too, with the blackout curtains drawn all the way back. The pale moonlight poured in through the windows like milk, drenching my walls, my desk, my rug like I was standing in a bowl of it.

I walked toward my bed. No one there. Nothing on it, either, except for a deflated bag of potato chips, a few crumbs spilling out on my quilt. I brushed them off onto the floor. We were never allowed to have food in our rooms. It was one of baba's rules.

"Yes?"

I turned around. She was behind me.

"Oh," I whispered. "Sorry." The girl's hair was wrapped into a bun, a few strands uncollected, glossy in the milk light. Her skin seemed to glow from the inside, like someone had placed a tea candle on her tongue and she balanced it there, behind her lips. She was wearing my pajamas, her round stomach poking out between the shirt and pants.

"Sleepwalking?" she asked.

I turned to leave.

"No," she said, and grabbed my wrist. "Stay. For a minute, I just—" She ran her hand through her hair, letting it down. "You're what, thirteen?" she asked, stepping closer to me, pushing a loose hair behind her ear.

"Twelve," I said, my voice smaller than I would have liked.

"Twelve," she repeated, trailing off. She looked down at her hand, still wrapped around my wrist. She let go. "Sorry. Didn't mean to grab you."

I looked at the door.

"Well, I'm you plus . . ." She counted in her head. "Plus nine." She laughed. "I know, I'm short. It makes me look younger than I am." She pressed her lips into a tight smile, her eyes boring into mine like a hook into a fish.

I pinched the rug between my toes. "My mom says it's good to look young."

"Well, your mom doesn't like me one bit, so . . ." She looked down at her stomach. "Oh!" she whispered. "I have an idea. Give me your hand."

"My hand?"

"Trust me."

"I don't know you."

"We live in the same house."

She took my hand. I let out a whimper.

"Loose, girl, loosen up," she said, shaking my hand until it was limp, then setting it on her stomach. Warm met cold.

"See? Nothing bad. Just life under there. Small life."

I pulled my hand back. "I'm going to go now."

I ran back to Rafa's room and climbed into his bed. It was one of our last nights living with baba and it ended like this: Rafa next to me, a stegosaurus, T. rex, and velociraptor in the space between us. Mama in our parents' bedroom. Baba on the couch. The girl in my room underneath my yellow patched quilt blooming me a half sister.

In the morning, I wake up a few minutes before the blare of mama's alarm. The sun is rising in the corner of the sky, so bright it is acidic, dripping sour light. I roll down my window and stick my head out, looking all the way to the left, then all the way to the right. No one there. I sit back, relieved. All around us, the leaves are changing color, like the city hired someone to paint them, little by little, overnight.

After I roll the window back up, I press my palm to it. It feels as thin as sugar glass. The wind rams up against the car, strong enough to shatter all the windows into shards, hundreds of small, jagged mirrors on our laps. No knocking needed. If this happened, I would ask mama when we would leave, and I know she would say "soon," like she always does. She would stare straight ahead, out the broken windshield, while ants swarmed our bodies, sugar-hungry. "Soon," she would say while they crawled into our mouths, pinpricking welts into our tongues with their stingers, their antenna heads poking out between our teeth.

At around three, while mama is finishing the second half of her shift, I join Rafa at the computers. He plays a video game set in space, shooting aliens with pink stardust, swerving a rocket to avoid meteors, and I open a blank document and make eight columns: address, rent amount, security deposit, number of bedrooms, number of bathrooms, utilities included, location, schools nearby. A template online recommends these categories. The computer is boxy and slow, the mouse lagging across the screen.

By the time mama ends her shift at five, I have a paper to show her. I scan our library card and use one of our twenty free pages to print it out. I hand it to her in front of the car while she rummages through her purse, looking for her keys.

"What's this?" she asks, holding it up. She squints her eyes as she reads it.

"I made it. It's a list."

Mama looks it over, her eyes scanning the columns. She nods and folds it up.

"Aren't you going to use it?" I ask.

"To do what?"

"To find an apartment."

"Mija, these are all out of our price range."

I swallow. "Okay, by how much?"

"Thank you," mama says, and pulls her keys out of her purse. "I can't think about this right now, okay?" She unlocks the car, clicking the button twice.

"Later?"

"Sure, later."

I cannot help it. "When?"

"Damn it, Sofia, I don't know when. I just got off work. I'm tired. I'm walking around in there all day, every day," she says, pointing in the direction of the clinic. "And what about you? What do *you* do all day besides read books?"

"That," I say, and point to the paper.

She crumples it up. This, I know, is not positive reinforcement.

I read the men in the waiting room sometimes. When mama has a night shift and we have to stay at the clinic until she clocks out at eight, I watch them walk in, check in, then sit down. The chairs are comfortable: speckled gray and foamy. I sink into mine, cross my hands over my lap, and wait. The receptionist's typing is as steady as a clock ticking. By now, Rafa has fallen asleep in his chair. When the door swings open, I look up, and if a man walks inside, I try and gauge whether or not he would be a good dad—or if his hands look too rough, his jaw set too mean, his voice too deep for him to be good. Mama says you can tell if someone has kids based on how many forehead wrinkles they have.

"Not by how many smile wrinkles?" I asked her once.

I remember her rolling her eyes, smiling. "I guess those count too."

Based on that calculation, some of the men who walk into the clinic have at least nine kids. But mama says having kids does not make you a dad, just a man with kids, and when she said that at dinner one time, standing over the stove while she ladled beef and green bean stew into our bowls, baba got up and slapped her.

The stew splattered everywhere. After he grabbed his keys and left, her fingertips hovered above the imprint on her cheek. “See what I mean?”

We nodded. We saw. It was red.

I steal a home-improvement magazine from the clinic. I read it in the car.

On page eleven, a cream-white flower pot. Forty-nine dollars. It promises clean living.

Page twenty-five, Egyptian cotton towels. I wonder what baba knows about that.

If it were up to me, I would pair the black-and-white arrowhead rug on page fourteen with the blue crushed velvet couch on page fifty-nine. For a "splash of color," as the magazine suggests every space needs. I look around our car—splashes of color everywhere. Shirts and straw wrappers and cups.

The industrial lamp on page twenty-two would add brightness to the room—orange light, not white, so it feels like I am standing before the sun. The candles on pages eight, nine, and in the corner of the room on page forty-three, everywhere around the house. Alight all day. Vanilla-scented. Matching plates (page thirty-six). Separate glass plates for salad (page thirty-seven). Knives and forks and spoons cut from sterling steel.

A room for each of us.

I show mama my favorite bedspread. Peach with white polka dots.

"Soon," she says. "Soon, okay?"

And I think this must be her favorite word.

She says it all the time, firmly, the one syllable.

When I am bored, I write it over and over again in my notebook. And when the pencil lead snaps, breaking off like a small gray tooth, I trace the word on the lined paper with my fingertips until I get drowsy:

soon soon soon soon soon soon soon soon soon soon soon soon
soon soon soon soon soon soon soon soon soon soon soon soon
soon soon soon soon soon soon soon soon soon soon soon soon
soon soon soon soon soon soon soon soon soon soon soon soon
soon soon soon soon soon soon soon soon soon soon soon soon
soon soon soon soon soon soon soon soon soon soon soon soon
soon soon soon soon soon soon soon soon soon soon soon soon
soon soon soon soon soon soon soon soon soon soon soon soon
soon soon soon soon soon soon soon soon soon soon soon soon
soon soon soon soon soon soon soon soon soon soon soon soon
soon soon soon soon soon soon soon soon soon soon soon soon
soon soon soon soon soon soon soon soon soon soon soon soon
soon soon soon soon soon soon soon soon soon soon soon soon
soon soon soon soon soon soon soon soon soon soon soon soon
soon soon soon soon soon soon soon soon soon soon soon soon
soon soon soon soon soon soon soon soon soon soon soon soon
soon soon soon soon soon soon soon soon soon soon soon soon
soon soon soon soon soon soon soon soon soon soon soon soon
soon soon soon soon soon soon soon soon soon soon soon soon
soon soon soon soon soon soon soon soon soon soon soon soon
soon soon soon soon soon soon soon soon soon soon soon soon
soon soon soon soon soon soon soon soon soon soon soon soon
soon soon soon soon soon soon soon soon soon soon soon soon
soon soon soon soon soon soon soon soon soon soon soon soon
soon soon soon soon soon soon soon soon soon soon soon soon
soon soon soon soon soon soon soon soon soon soon soon soon
soon soon soon soon soon soon soon soon soon soon soon soon
soon soon soon soon soon soon soon soon soon soon soon soon
soon soon soon soon soon soon soon soon soon soon soon soon
soon soon soon soon soon soon soon soon soon soon soon soon

It passes the time.

A week before Thanksgiving, mama has a theory.

"I don't know," she says, pressing her phone to her ear. "Maybe she got stuck on his eyes like I did." She looks out the window. The dusk is lavender, a whole field of it sprouting from the dark soil of the horizon. She is on the phone with Angela, my friend Lena's mom, who has called to ask why we have not responded to the wedding invitation she mailed to our house last week. If things were normal, I know mama would say something like, "Because it's your third wedding in two years." Then she would turn to me and say, "Poor Lena. All those dads."

I want to ask if I can talk to Lena. It has been almost a month since I have seen her. I rest my head on the seat belt strap, imagining her and Chloe at the restaurant by the ocean where we had reservations for Chloe's birthday. Every year, Chloe's mom orders a whole bright red lobster for herself and three baskets of coconut shrimp for me, Lena, and Chloe. I imagine the chocolate-raspberry cake. The twelve lit candles, specks of red and orange and yellow caught in all of our eyes.

We receive calls like this often, mostly parents from school calling to ask why they have not seen mama at the PTA meetings, why their kids' birthday party invitations have gone unanswered, why our names are not on the roster for next season's volleyball team. Why their kids have not seen us in class. Is someone sick? One by one, she calls them back and tells them we are having a Family Emergency, leaving it at that, and they gasp and sympathize, then ask for our new address, and mama says we will send it to them soon.

"But, Nina." I hear Angela's muffled voice sigh. "Does it matter why?"

"It's just that she's so young," she says.

"How young?"

"Twenty-one. Barely."

"Jesus, what an asshole."

Mama sits forward in her seat. "And to think that he let her into our home. What was I supposed to do? I didn't want to yank the kids from school, but I had to. He got so angry the morning we left. So angry. I mean, he hit Rafa," mama says, scratching her forehead. "I just didn't want him to be able to find us after that, you know? I don't trust him anymore. I don't."

"I think you did the right thing, leaving when you did. But why not stay with someone in the meantime? I'm sure—"

"We're not doing that," she says, shaking her head. "When people find out about these things, they treat you differently. I've seen it happen."

A few seconds pass. "What about your dad?"

"No way," mama says. "You know that."

"Are they back in school yet?" Angela asks.

She grows quiet. "Not yet. I'm still looking for one."

I tug on mama's elbow. "Can I talk to Lena?"

She puts her finger to her mouth then walks out of the car to finish the call.

Mama explains it to me this way. She has reached out to an organization that helps people pay their rent. For us to qualify for their help, we would need to have missed a few months' worth of payments once we get an apartment. Then, with Proof of Need established, they would swoop in and give us Financial Relief. Which she says they say will help us. Mama says we turned in our Preliminary Paperwork earlier this morning with a few clicks at the library computer. Their office will close for Thanksgiving in three days, on Wednesday. She hopes they will get back to us before then.

I tap my pencil to my chin. Above us, the blue afternoon hazes over the sunroof. "But wouldn't it be bad to miss rent payments?"

"I'm not asking what you think." She sighs. "God, why do I bother? Why can't you just listen?" she says, turning the keys in the ignition. The car hums awake.

I look down at my journal, sliding the yellow pencil down through the metal spiral. "I was, though."

"Just read your book, okay?"

"I was." I tap my fingers on the armrest, the vinyl wrinkled like elephant skin. I do not want to feel annoyed, but I am, heat pricking the back of my neck.

Mama makes a *tth* sound with her mouth. Sometimes, when she gets like this, I watch her get madder and madder like a firecracker that lights itself. "Watch it."

"You watch it," I say quietly.

She leans forward. "What was that?"

"Nothing."

On mama's birthday, the physician's assistant, one of the people who hired her, said she remembered that mama had a November birthday when she reviewed her application. "But I didn't realize it was right around the corner," the physician's assistant said when the afternoon shift ended, guiding mama by the elbow into the break room, where the nurses, receptionist, and janitor stood behind a white frosted cake, a single candle in the middle glowing blue and yellow. The nurse practitioner stood in the corner, holding a balloon that said "Happy" in gold lettering.

"The one that said 'Birthday' flew away," one of the other nurses said, and pointed out the window.

After they sang "Happy Birthday" and mama blew out the candle, they served her a slice—cinnamon cake with a peach-and-spice filling, she tells me and Rafa now. She reaches toward the passenger seat, grabs two foil-wrapped paper plates, and hands them to us in the back seat.

Rafa removes the foil from his plate to see a slice lying on its side, brown specks of cinnamon in the cake, the globs of peach oozing out from the filling. Mama hands us two clear plastic forks.

"Happy birthday, mama," I say, lifting the foil off my plate.

Rafa nods, eating a mouthful of cake. "Happy birthday." He reaches for his water bottle, almost knocking mine off the cup holder.

"Careful," I say.

Rafa takes a sip of water then looks up at mama. "So, what do you do in there, anyway?"

"In the clinic?"

He holds up his plate. "Do you have cake every day?"

Mama laughs, shakes her head. "I do lots of things," she says, describing the swabbing, the weighing, the temperature-taking, the immunizations.

"Immunizations?" Rafa says.

"Shots," mama says, and pokes his shoulder with her index finger, making a *pst* sound, imitating a needle.

"Oh." He rubs his arm. "Ow."

Mama told me once that when she was younger, she wanted to become a doctor, the kind that delivers babies, but decided to apply to nursing school instead. "And then what happened?" I asked her. "I had you two," she said simply.

"Any babies today?" I ask.

"What?"

"At the clinic."

"No, not today."

Later tonight, when we have dinner, plastic bowls of ramen we filled with boiling water in the grocery store, mama does not have any, saying one of the patients brought a basket full of nectarines to the clinic in the morning and that plus the cake meant she was not hungry for dinner. I look up at her. She said the same thing yesterday: a patient brought a cooler full of tamales and a tray of cookies for the staff. She was not hungry for dinner then, either. I imagine the cooler, steaming with the red tamales, the green ones. A whole tray of sugar cookies on the table and crumbs like glitter on everyone's lips.

"You sure?" I ask, because I could have sworn I heard her stomach growling earlier.

"I'm sure," she says. "You two go ahead."

On Tuesday, the shelves at the market are almost empty. The last few cans of green beans look as flattened as stomped-on soda cans, some with labels torn off the side like a ripped dress. The smooth metal gleams underneath, exposed like bare skin. When Rafa asks if we are doing anything special for Thanksgiving, we are standing in front of the granola bars, mama handing them to me box by box as I stack them in the cart. The coupon book in the basket says they are "Buy Three, Get Two Free."

"Are we, mama?" he asks.

"It depends."

"On what?"

I want to ask if we could go to abuelo's house for Thanksgiving, like we used to before, when he would crouch down by the oven, use his oven mitts to pull out the turkey, and let me baste the crispy brown skin. He let me light the braided candlesticks when we sat down for dinner, helping me click the lighter until it sparked. The last time we went, Rafa was so little, mama set him on the kitchen counter and he grabbed the soap dispenser shaped like an apple by the sink and bit into it, thinking it was real. I want to ask if I can borrow her phone—maybe I can call abuelo myself. But mama has been checking her phone every few minutes, waiting for the rent relief agency to call. So I arrange the boxes of granola bars in the cart and keep quiet.

"On whether the organization can help us in time. I'm supposed to hear back from them today," she says, stopping the cart in front of the candy section. She picks up a pack of jelly beans, shakes it, and it sounds like pebbles spilling out onto the floor. She flips the box around to look for the price and then puts it in the cart. "Check to see if this is on sale, too, mija?"

After we check out—five boxes of granola bars, three water bottles, six bananas, and one box of half-price jelly beans with the receipt in the bag—noon comes around and mama still has not heard back, so she dials the agency's number on her phone and tells us to hush. "And don't listen," she says, but of course we do. I grab two bananas from the passenger seat and give one to Rafa.

She asks if she could borrow my journal in case she needs to write something down. I hand it to her. When she points to a pen on the floor, I hand her that, too, dusting it off on my pants first.

They answer.

Mama says she is calling to send over the final set of paperwork, and what do they prefer, fax or email? But the person on the other end tells her there is no need for that.

"Sorry, I'm not following," mama says, clicking her pen with her thumb, then scribbling something down.

"Consider yourself lucky," I hear a tired voice say. "They weren't doing any good here."

"I'm sorry, who is this? I'm trying to reach—"

"I know who you're trying to reach. We've been getting calls like this all day. They're not in business anymore—they were never in business."

“Well, who can I—”

“Goodbye,” the voice says, and hangs up.

Mama looks at her phone, stunned. “Shit,” she says, pounding her fist on the steering wheel. “Shit shit fucking shit.”

She grips the steering wheel hard, her knuckles popping out like almonds, then bends down, placing her forehead on the face of the steering wheel. Hearing her sniffling, I can tell she is crying. I reach into the center compartment for a handful of napkins, place them on her lap, then point at a skateboarder outside Rafa’s window to distract him.

The windows are like TV screens, each one its own show. On Rafa's screen, the skateboarder swerves to avoid a paletero, who curses in Spanish, pushing the cart over an uneven crack in the sidewalk. A tiny bell rings. On mine, a girl sneezes and a white-haired woman, maybe her grandmother, reaches into her purse to hand her a tissue. The girl thanks her. There is no off button, no mute, no skips. There is only the rattle of grocery carts as they are returned, the puff and whiff of a blond lady's sour rose perfume, a parent stooping down to scold a child: "No, Lucy, don't you dare, we are in public." I lean my head on the seat belt, watching the cast of characters act.

After a few minutes, mama straightens herself out, folding down the mirror to fix her hair. She rips out the sheet of paper she used to write something down on, then hands me my journal—or she is about to, but then she takes it back. "You've really filled this up, haven't you?" she says, flipping through it.

"Yeah," I say. "Wait, don't."

"What is this?" she asks, the journal open to the page of Soon.

"Give it back."

She has my journal on her lap. When I reach for it, she pulls it away. She looks out the windshield. "That's not normal," she says, to me or to herself, I cannot tell.

"It's mine," I say. "Give it back."

She angles herself away from me, flipping through the pages.

"You can't read my journal. It's mine," I say, desperate. I want to cry or scream, or both.

She places the journal on her seat and then sits on it.

"It's mine," I say, trying to pull it out from underneath her.

"I paid for it," mama says.

"Baba paid for it."

"Baba paid for it," she repeats, exasperated, her hands in the air. Her eyebrows tighten, as if someone has pulled a string that sews them tight together. She opens her door, grabs my journal, then walks to the front of the market. She stops in front of the trash can and throws the journal inside. So hard, the trash can teeters.

I am so mad, I do not know what to do with it, do not know where to put it—I feel it in my chest, then my hands, my fists. I look around the car, then grab her phone from the cup holder. I throw it out the window, hard.

Rafa's lip starts to quiver. "What did you do?"

"It's okay," I say a few minutes later, taking Rafa by the elbow and pulling him closer to me. I smooth over his hair, soft and curly and brown, then comb it forward with my fingers.

The phone is fine. Not even a crack on the screen. I look at mama screaming, her forehead on the horn, honking it. We are standing outside of the car. It feels safer out here. A woman, the one with white hair from earlier, walks up to me and asks me if everything is all right.

I nod. "Thank you."

She walks away, uncertain.

I walk to the trash can just as a man tosses a salad into it, followed by a red can of soda. I reach in, hold my breath, and feel around for my journal. By the time I find it, a short line has formed behind me.

"Sorry," I say, then move out of the way. The journal is covered in ranch dressing, dripping with soda. It smells so bad I throw it out anyway. I wipe my hands on my pants, then regret it.

I wait for it to be over, for the honking to stop, for mama to say, tiredly, "Just get in, all right?" her voice spent, her head low, her face like a candle with the light snuffed out of it, dim, the sky dim, too, because it has started to rain. Her lunch break is over, she tells us. She drops us off at the library then drives to the clinic.

Mama drives us to the beach after work. "The waves help me think," she tells us. When we get there, no one is in the water, or on the sand, or in the parking lot. It is still raining. The clouds have bleached the sunlight out of the day.

"Want to play I Spy?" I ask Rafa.

"Not really," he says, reaching under his seat for a dinosaur.

Looking out the window, I spy water droplets sliding down, leaving glossy snail-like trails on the glass. I spy the crinkled sun-cracked vinyl of the steering wheel. A blue air freshener shaped like a wave dangles from the mirror. Ocean Mist. Mama got it from the gas station last week because it was on sale. "Only fifty cents." Up close it smells like coconuts and sunscreen and salt.

Outside, on the promenade, dead red leaves whirl around themselves on the concrete: a red tango. I spy seagulls coasting through the air like paper airplanes, wide-winged, circling the dock with mouths full of fish, gray tails arched over the side of their beaks. The scales refract rainbow light. There is the slow, sequined movement of the ocean, its glittery sway. Then when the sun goes down, everything is honey gold until the sky shutters off, black and wet.

"Did it work?" Rafa asks her on the drive to tonight's parking lot. "Were you able to think?"

"I think so," she says.

That night I wake up to the click of the car door opening.

Mama is looking for something on the passenger side and the way she is doing it, putting one foot over the center storage compartment, then another, I can tell she is trying to make as little noise as possible. We are parked outside of a building with a sign that has a red neon light twisted into the number six. It hangs over a blue background, the word "Motel" turned on its side. The highway is nearby, the loud rush of cars crackling in the air like thick static.

We have parked here for the last three nights. The front half of the car is illuminated by the white light shining down at an angle from the streetlamp. If there is such a thing as neon white, this is it, right here. It is like someone has fixed a spotlight on us, only us. Mama said this was the only parking space left. "The lights turn off automatically at ten anyway," she said a few hours ago.

I rub my eyes. It is nine fifteen.

On our second night here, when Rafa asked her why we kept parking by the motel—he liked to choose where we went—she applied berry lipstick in the fold-down mirror, pressed her lips together to rub it in, and said it was because the motel has a bathroom. "I'll be right back," she said yesterday, but it took hours until she returned to the car.

This time she has a small flat square in her hand. Its crinkly plastic catches in the light before she shoves it into one of her pockets.

When she closes the door, I wake up Rafa.

"She left."

"What?" he asks, alarmed.

"Mama left."

He rubs his eyes. "Where?"

"I guess she's going inside," I say, pointing to the lobby. I shrug his head off my shoulder and move from the back seat to the passenger seat, craning my neck to see her outline move vaguely in the dark. "Maybe she's using the bathroom."

I reach to open the door but stop, my fingers on the handle. The car alarm would go off if I opened it. I can already see mama's face in front of mine, hot-breathed, wild-eyed, asking why I did not stay put like I was supposed to. I recline my seat and decide to keep watch instead.

About thirty minutes later, after Rafa falls back asleep, his breath raspy, hushed, I see mama walking toward the car and a tall figure, probably a man, walking in the opposite direction, away from us.

"She's coming back."

Rafa wakes up.

I get a good look at her as she makes her way over to the car. The skin around her nose looks damp and oily. Her hair, usually tied back neatly in a ponytail, is up in a bun, a nest of brown curls on top of her head. A small feather sticks out. Standing at her door, she undoes her bun and shakes out her hair, letting it fall down to her collarbone, flowy, frizzy. Mama unlocks the car and makes her way inside. The feather below her ear like an earring.

"You're back," I say.

She gasps, looking at the both of us. She smells a little like smoke, like incense. "You scared me."

"Where'd you go?" Rafa asks.

"Nope, no questions. Bedtime."

Out of habit, Rafa makes his way to her from the back seat and gives her his forehead for a bedtime kiss. Mama pauses, shakes her head, turns away from him, opens the door, then throws up. She wipes her mouth with the back of her hand and then uses a napkin to rub it clean, and even then, a sour yellow-green smell lingers outside her lips like a whisper.

"Air kiss." She blows one in his direction. He catches it with his hands.

Sometimes, when I am sitting here in the dark cell of the car and the streetlights flicker from yellow to red to green, and the stick-figure man on the digital crosswalk sign shines his white fluorescent skin, and the orange pixel numbers count down from twenty to ten to one, I think of my bedroom and how dark it got there—no light except the soft glow of the hallway night-light pooling like oil underneath the door.

If it is dark enough, I let baba into the car. He is sitting in the passenger seat with his head turned toward me. Baba with the swipe of beige on his jeans, paint caught in his knuckle hairs like small patches of wheat. I can see the stubble on his chin, the way it stretches down to his neck. He is wearing a gray sweater. His fingernails grip the armrest, and he is asking me, quietly, when we are coming back.

He tells me to call him. If I tell him where we are, he can pick us up. He starts to tell me his phone number. He wants me to write it down.

In the months before the girl moved in, baba spent hours on the phone, the ringlet cord of the landline draped over his shoulder. We did not know who he was talking to or what to make of it, his voice suddenly sweeter, like someone poured honey into his mouth. When Rafa and I peeked into his office, we would find him reclined all the way back on his swivel chair, smiling into the receiver. Running his hand through his hair as he looked up at the ceiling.

"Was that teta?" I asked once, after he was in there for almost three hours.

He cleared his throat, rubbing his neck. "Yes, it was."

"How is she?"

"The same, habibi."

On those nights, when mama knew she would be coming home late from a PTA meeting, she would make something for dinner the night before and put it in the refrigerator for us to heat up the next day—green enchiladas, chicken and rice, bean-and-cheese burritos. This time, though, mama left a note on the kitchen counter, a piece of printer paper folded into a tent saying she placed ingredients by the stove for the three of us to make dinner: fettuccine Alfredo. Her cousin just had twins, and she would be gone for the weekend, flying to another state to help them. Baba picked up the note, crumpled it, then tossed it into the trash can.

"Okay, then," he said. "Are you hungry?"

"I'm starving," Rafa said.

"You're not starving, Rafa," he said, annoyed. "Don't exaggerate." He held up the box of pasta, turning it over to find the instructions. "Okay. Where does she keep the pots?"

I pointed to the cabinet to the right of the sink.

When the water began to boil, we poured the fettuccine into the pot and set a timer. Ten minutes later, when the timer went off, baba helped me drain it into a colander in the sink, thick, pale steam rising from the noodles, the sauce simmering in a shallow pot on the stove. When I removed the lid to check on the sauce, a boiling bubble popped, a splash of white landing on baba's shirt.

"Careful, you're making a mess," he said, looking down at the spot. "Where are the towels?"

"In the drawer."

"This one?"

"Yeah."

"Don't say 'yeah.' It sounds bad. Say 'yes, baba.'"

"Yes, baba."

"Is it almost done?" Rafa asked, piercing the air with his fork, then slamming it down on the table, the metal clanking hard on the granite.

"Almost done," I said, taking the fork from him.

Baba got a bowl for each of us, using tongs to pull out pasta noodles that were limp and long like wet blond hair. He used a ladle to pour sauce on top. Reaching into the spice cabinet, he found a bottle of dried parsley and sprinkled a pinch of it over each bowl. "Like they do at the restaurants," he said, patting Rafa on the back after. "I'm going to eat in my office. You two be good."

Before we left, mama and baba tried marriage counseling to see if there was anything left to fix. In late October, a week or so after the girl moved in, I overheard mama whispering on the phone, telling someone that she thought she could still change baba's mind. With the right counselor, she thought he could be convinced to ask the girl to leave, she whispered. I watched Rafa while they were out at these appointments, hauling his textbooks out of his backpack and washing grapes in a small tin bowl for his after-school snack. I poured him a glass of milk. Added two ice cubes inside, the way he liked. The girl only came out of my room to use the bathroom. With both mama and baba gone, this is when I had the most authority.

"Better eat all those grapes," I warned Rafa, the way mama would.

And he did. He ate all of them.

Baba said he did not want to try marriage counseling because he did not want some American lady asking him about his personal life. So mama found an Egyptian therapist and reluctantly, with loud, suffering sighs, he agreed to go. At the time, I wanted to ask her why she insisted on these appointments, why she cried for them, begging. I heard the crashing of plates in the kitchen enough times, put my hands over my ears to muffle the shouting, the crying, the wild hyena laughing after, to know exactly when Rafa and I should hide in our rooms with our backs pressed to the doors.

When they got home from their first appointment, mama walked through the front door flushed, tears dotting her lower lashes like drops of resin. Baba walked in with good posture, his chest puffed out slightly, smiling. Rafa and I were sitting on the couch. The keys jingled as baba hung them on a hook by the door. The click of the lock in the latch.

"See, some of it's just a cultural thing, like she said," baba said as he slipped off his shoes.

"That's not what she said. At all. That over there"—she pointed to my room—"and this whole thing, this whole situation has to do with you and you only. It's you. You did this," she said, jabbing a finger into his chest. "And if I called your mom and told her what you did, she would be on my side. My side. So don't try and blame it on anything else. Fucking asshole." She threw her purse on the couch. If mama called teta, she would not know what to say. She does not speak Arabic. And teta does not speak English. I imagined the two of them on the phone, saying nothing, the line crackling.

"You're not calling her."

"I never said I was, but *if*—"

"Are you threatening me?"

"I'm not threatening you."

"I'm leaving," he said, lacing up his shoes again, reaching for the keys.

"Careful out there," mama said, letting out a laugh. "We don't have any more bedrooms left."

When he came back that night, I walked into the kitchen to get a glass of water. He was sitting on the armchair in the glow of the flower lamp, each bulb a different color. Blue, pink, and violet light laying itself over his face, his hands, his pants. I was too far away from him to tell if he was crying, but then he rubbed his eyes and reached forward, toward the coffee table, for a napkin. He blew his nose, then dropped the tissue, limp, a flag, on his lap. Then he switched off the light.

The day we left, it all happened so quickly. When mama told him to back away, that we were leaving, baba hardly looked at us. We were on the front lawn, the grass in dry yellow patches by the brick walkway. The white roses mama planted in the spring were browning at the edges. I had my history project on ancient revolutions in my right hand. When I set it down on the lawn to help mama with our bags, the wind blew it in baba's direction, and he walked over to hand it to me. Mama dropped the bag she was stuffing into the trunk and rushed over, standing between us with her arms up, telling him to back away.

A few minutes earlier, when baba was on the phone in the kitchen, nodding as he scribbled something on a page in a notebook, Rafa was reaching across the table for a cereal box when he knocked over a glass of orange juice with his elbow. It was an accident. But the juice spilled all over a stapled stack of baba's papers, all over his notebook, too, smudging the black ink. There was the sharp, sour-sweet tang of oranges. The pulp scattered across the tablecloth.

Then the scuffle of chairs. Baba grabbed Rafa's face. Mama walked into the room and asked what fell, then pulled Rafa away from him. Baba charged toward him anyway, pushing her back, toppling a chair over. I stood in the corner with my hands over my ears. Then the snap of the wood, mama telling me to get into the car, pounding on baba's chest, saying, "You promised you'd never do this. You promised."

In the car, mama locked the doors. She said "shh" to Rafa, telling him he was fine, and could he just hold still for a second, please? "Let me see."

"Don't talk to me," she said to baba when he came up to the car after she had put the last of the bags in the trunk. The girl peered out of our front door holding a pink robe shut across her belly. Mama's robe. She waved at me.

"I'm sorry," baba said to Rafa, reaching to hug him from the side.

"Don't you touch them."

Rafa looked at me, unsure, caught between the two of them. I nodded. He hugged baba back.

"I'm sorry, okay, habibi?" Then he turned to me. "Sofia," he said, reaching for me. "I'll see you soon, okay?"

I held my breath as he hugged me.

"Come on, kids."

After a second or so, he let go of me, of us. And we drove.

Thanksgiving dinner is two granola bars for each of us, and after we finish them, we recline the seats and lie down with our growling bellies pointed up at the car ceiling. Mama's sounds more like a gurgle, Rafa's more like a splat, and mine, a curly, coiled sound with its own echo. The crumbs that have landed on the floor look as if someone scattered them there to feed birds, the way the women in visors do while sitting cross-legged on park benches, sipping coffee. Mama says we need to make the granola bars last until she gets her paycheck in two weeks. "Just a few at a time, okay?"

I look at mama's phone. It would be so easy for her to call someone and ask to borrow some money, even ten, fifteen dollars, for dinner today. The phone sits untouched in the cup holder.

"Oh, the jelly beans!" she says a minute later. "I forgot about them. Sit up, sit up."

She says she had these as a kid, that she and her cousins would sit in a circle on the cold tile floor of her tía's kitchen while the adults played lotería. She reaches into the center divider and pulls out the pack of jelly beans, shaking them. "I love that sound." She lifts the top flap of the cardboard box open and explains that, when combined, the jelly beans make Thanksgiving dinner. She pours out a few into her palm. The brown one is supposed to taste like turkey, the white one like mashed potatoes, the green one like peas, the purple one like cranberry sauce, and the orange one like pumpkin pie. "Ready?" she asks. "Let's do the turkey one first. The main course."

We each take a brown jelly bean from her palm and place them on our tongues.

"One, two, three."

We bite down.

It tastes like wet cardboard. A little like a Communion wafer, that one time we had it at church. Rafa scrunches up his face, reaches for a napkin, then spits it out. "That's gross, mama," he says. "Which one next?"

Mama is laughing, covering her mouth. "Let's wash it down with some mashed potatoes." She reaches for the box.

We go through all of them, the white, the brown, the green, the purple, the orange. Main course, sides, and dessert. A full feast. Mama laughs so hard, tears stream down her face, her nose stuffy, too, and I want to hold this moment in my hands. To put it to my ear like a conch shell. This is what mama's laugh sounds like. Wiping her eyes with the sleeve of her sweater, she says that on some Thanksgivings, it is okay not to be thankful for anything, but that this is not one of them.

"Maybe I could get a job," I say the next day. All around us the sunset glows orange and pink, a layer of fresh acrylic paint over the sky. If I get a job I could save up for a brand-new watercolor set, the kind with twenty-four colors, and maybe a pack of canvases, a paintbrush or two. But I worry that any paint, even a single drop of it, is enough to remind mama of baba, and then what would happen? I roll down the window. Right outside a honey bee lands on a yellow petal of a daffodil, weighing it down.

"You're a student. That's your job," mama says. "And besides, you're too young."

"But I'm not in school."

"I'm working on it."

"But I can at least apply."

"I said I'm working on it."

We are parked outside the grocery store. I could work there, in the bakery, piping chocolate frosting onto cupcakes. It might even be fun, might be kind of like painting. In the summer, I would stick American flags into sheet cakes for Fourth of July, scatter star-shaped sprinkles along the borders. In the fall, I would frost orange cupcakes into pumpkins and use black icing for the jack-o'-lantern smiles. In the winter: gingerbread men, cookies decorated like wreaths, candy canes, and Christmas trees. I would put on an apron. I look down at my arms. I can easily carry bags of flour.

Or I could bag groceries. Mama taught me how. The things that should go in the fridge should go together—milk, yogurt, butter—cans distributed by weight, double-bagged to avoid ripping. Eggs in their own bag, bananas on top so they do not get bruised, although mama says the bruises are sugar, the sweetest parts. But people prefer bananas that look like the ones in the advertisements, like they are dipped in yellow. So, on top they will go.

"I'm gonna use the bathroom," I say, then unlock the door and walk toward the market.

Inside, by the bread, is a small table with a picnic tablecloth draped over it, a balloon tied to one of the legs. The balloon says "Hiring!," its circular shadow landing on a folder with the market logo. I open it. It is full of job applications. I take one. The application asks for: name, phone number, age, and desired role. I circle "Bakery Associate." I add six years to my age and then, easy, I am an adult. I list mama's phone number and email and leave the application on the table, tucked underneath the folder.

Outside the church across the street, the three of us stand under rain that seems unsure of itself, landing lightly on our hair, misting our foreheads. The church has a sad face—two blue stained-glass windows as round as eyes, blurred with rain. The wooden beams curve down like eyebrows. Mama hurries us inside, looking down at her wristwatch. It is Sunday.

"Sometimes there's lunch," she whispers, "after the service."

We walk into the church's narrow, humid mouth. Inside, the pews are lined up like rows of brown teeth and the carpet, a long red felt tongue, unfurls down the middle. We take our seats in the back. So far back, the priest is only a voice booming through the rectangular speakers mounted on the wall. A sweeping green robe. The Eucharist, when he holds it up, is a tan speck I have to squint to see. We stand, then sit, then kneel, doing what everyone else does. From above, we might look like windup toys, all of us.

The priest motions for us to sit down.

This church could not be more different from the one back home—St. Peter's, a Coptic Orthodox Church a few blocks away from the highway—where we would leave home at six in the morning without eating breakfast so the first thing we ate would be the orbana at Communion. There, men sat on the left side of the church, women on the right. All of the girls and women had to cover their hair with white lacy veils, which we tied into knots under our chins so they would stay in place. The priest delivered the sermon in both English and Arabic. At Communion, the men went first, then the women, all of us drinking from the same gold chalice, abouna lifting a long spoon to our lips, the sudden tartness of the wine. It tasted nothing like grapes.

I look to my left and see a man in a tan suit help his daughter out of a turtleneck sweater, lifting it up over her head then folding it and setting it down on the pew, and I wonder if baba is still going to church and, if he is, what he is telling his friends about where we are. "They're at Rafa's basketball game," I can hear him whisper during the sermon. Or "Sofia has the flu."

"Again?" they would say.

He would nod. "Again."

When the service ends, the priest adjusts the microphone and mentions a fundraiser for the school next door, a private elementary-middle school the church is affiliated with, saying they need a new playground. There are flyers at the back, by the holy water, in case anyone is interested in donating, he says.

The priest steps down from the lectern, adjusts his green robe, centers the gold cross over his chest, and walks toward the back of the church, greeting people with a wave, shaking their hands, when he stops a few feet in front of us and locks eyes with mama. He looks around. Then he continues walking with his mouth slightly open, and then, as if realizing it is open, closes it, pink lip to pink lip. An altar boy taps him on the shoulder. Mama picks up her purse. The priest excuses himself from the boy, smiling and saying sorry, just a second, and walks toward us. But mama, she has us by the elbows and we are out of there. "Time to go," she whispers.

I want to turn around to look, but she tells us to keep walking. The priest follows us outside to a patch of sunflowers unfurling by the entrance, where there is no one except an older couple crossing the street away from the church, toward the parking lot. It is still raining. The dirt around the sunflowers, wet as mud.

"Excuse me," he says, and leans closer to us. His green robe leans too. "Sarah?" he whispers.

"I didn't know you were a priest," mama whispers back, then takes us and continues walking.

We cross the street.

Just then, the parishioners start filing out of the church in their sundresses and suits, their button-downs and pleated skirts, and put on their raincoats, pop open their umbrellas. We find our car in the parking lot.

"Who's Sarah?" Rafa says, strapping his seat belt over his lap. I turn around to face the church. The priest is still there, waving goodbye to parishioners. He takes an umbrella that someone offers to him, holds it over his head, and straightens out his collar, still watching us. We drive away, leaving him there, a leaf in the wind.

When the grocery store calls on Monday morning to set up an interview, mama pulls her phone away from her face to look at it, as if the phone itself confuses her. "You have the wrong person," she says, then hangs up.

A second later mama turns around. "Unless," she says. "Did you? You didn't."

"Did what?" I ask. It is better this way.

She shakes her head. "Never mind."

On her lunch break, she calls the church and asks to speak to the priest. She stays on hold for three minutes, violin then trumpet then piano spewing out of the speakerphone, staticky, then steps out of the car, into the rain, when he picks up.

Sometime early Tuesday morning, mama wakes up frenzied, maybe mid-dream, and tries opening her door, pulling, pushing, banging, even though it is locked. A small "damn it" slips from her, but her eyes dart over, and I pretend to be asleep, unhearing her. Mama is unheard. She tells us to wake up.

"Sofia, Rafa, come on."

I pretend to wake up, yawning. "What time is it?"

"The morning."

She tells us she has decided to sell her wedding ring. "It's broken anyway," she says, although it looks perfectly intact to me—a shiny knot of diamond. When she turns it in her fingers, a rainbow lands on my thigh like new, striped fabric over my jeans.

I look at mama's wrist, at the gold bracelet she always wears. She wears it so often, I am sure it has left an imprint, a trail of small teeth markings around her wrist. The bracelet, which baba got her after Rafa was born, has a small opal and an amethyst, me and Rafa's birthstones. Each as small as a lentil. When she gets nervous, she rolls the bracelet around her wrist, then stops, checks that the two stones are still there, and folds her hands in front of her.

"Are you selling that too?" I point to the bracelet.

"What, this?" says mama, touching the two stones. "Of course not."

I nod.

"And, mija?"

"Yes?"

"You'll get to go back to school again. A new one. You, too, Rafa."

When we show up on our first day, we are showered, uniformed, wrinkle-free. Our shirts, thick as a quilt, say "Holy Heart Catholic School" on the breast pocket with a tiny cross stitched in the corner. Rafa and I both wear a tie—him, long slacks, and me, a plaid skirt—and the word "scholarship" breaches like a bird in the canopy of adult conversation overhead, and so does mama's "thank you." Mama paid twenty dollars for each shirt, twenty-five for the pants, and thirty for the skirt. "Be careful," she told us yesterday, handing cash to the clerk at the uniform store. "We'll hang them up as soon as we get in the car so they stay nice and ironed."

Unlike at our old school, there is a crucifix in every room. Even one nailed above the window in the girls' bathroom. Slightly crooked, I notice, when the vice principal shows us around.

"We just ask that you go to church on Sundays," a lady with short bangs who introduces herself as Ms. Monique tells us, pointing in the direction of the cathedral with her cane. "And spread the word when you can."

"Of course. Won't we, kids?"

"In the meantime, these are for you."

Ms. Monique turns around, leans her cane against her desk

chair, and grabs a large cardboard box. "Just some blankets and snacks to keep you going. There's an envelope in there with a few vouchers for the grocery store, if you need them. Couple of gift cards in there for gas too."

"Thank you. Really," mama says, and takes the box from Ms. Monique. Rafa lifts a flap to peek inside.

Ms. Monique shrugs, her shoulders up to her ears. "Wasn't me. Father Charles insisted."

I think about what we must look like when mama leaves—a sixth grader with her first-grade brother holding her hand, smelling of mint because we showered at a gym and they had peppermint body soap in the showers and spearmint tea in the lobby. Mama signed up for a weeklong free trial, smiling at a camera for a membership photo before signing guest pass waivers for me and Rafa with a purple pen. When we leave Ms. Monique's office, a pantyhosed woman, the principal, calls us into the school and says it is warmer inside, handing us each a bagel. Rafa starts to cry. The principal has us stay in her office until the bell rings, where a beanbag twice the size of Rafa lies in the corner. He plops onto it, sprawls out like a starfish. He eats his bagel, the entire thing. I do too. Every sesame seed.

When it is eight o'clock, the principal walks me to the sixth-grade classroom after we drop Rafa off at his. "Good luck," I whisper, touching his shoulder.

The principal knocks on the door before opening it. When we step inside, twenty or so students look up, in the middle of unloading their backpacks. I straighten my skirt. The principal says she wants everyone's attention. She has an announcement to make.

"We have a new student joining us," she says, and bends down to me. "Want to introduce yourself, honey?"

"Sofia," I say, and my face grows hot. "I'm Sofia."

The teacher, Ms. Clyde, points to a seat in the back of the classroom, a blue chair with four silver bolts in the back, the same silver as the legs. My backpack lands near the foot of my chair in an empty sag. Quietly, she asks me where the rest of my school supplies are, if I left them in the office. I tell her I do not have any.

"Well, all right," she says.

"I'm sorry," I say.

"No need to apologize."

There are five rows of four desks, the students sitting boy-girl-boy-girl. A map of the United States is pinned into the bulletin board closest to me with gold thumbtacks, the American flag covering a corner of the map. I hear a low buzzing sound and look to my left. My seat is by the fish tank. There is a magenta betta fish nibbling on a plastic plant, murmuring bubbles to itself. When I lean closer, my nose pressed to the glass, it swims away, its tail a flag flowing in the water.

I take out my pencil. From back here, the teacher, in her brown cardigan and white dress, her slim arms hanging by her sides, looks like a mannequin from the mall.

"Okay," she says. "Let's pick up where we left off yesterday."

After the bell rings, just before recess, Ms. Clyde asks me to stay a few minutes before heading outside. I wait by her desk, where a heart-leaved plant trails down the side, potted next to a frizzy fern sprouting up like a fountain. A straw with a red lipstick stain pokes out of a gallon-size water bottle.

"I have someone I would like you to meet, Sofia," the teacher says.

She gestures to a girl behind her with her hair pulled up tight into a ponytail, the same plaid from our uniform on top of her head in a bow.

"Hi," the girl says. "I'm Ana." *This is Ana*, I think, and try to remember the name. I look at Ms. Clyde, who has already made her way back to her desk, straightening out a stack of papers. When Ana stretches out her hand to shake mine, I see it. I look up and see her trying to understand herself—looking at me, seeing a mirror. Ana is brown too.

Ana and I go outside, where yellow lines intersect into hopscotches and metal benches line the edge of the playground by the gate. There are kids sitting—on the benches, in a circle near the hopscotches, on top of the monkey bars—kids running, chasing volleyballs. And there is Ana and there is me, walking around it, tracing it out like a perimeter, length times width.

"Do you want some grapes?" she asks me, unzipping a plastic bag full of them, the stem poking through. "They're frozen. My dad likes them that way."

"Thanks," I say, and take the handful of them that she gives me, putting one in my mouth. I bite down. The grape breaks in a crunch. Sweet and cold.

"So, what kind of shows do you watch?"

I eat another grape. "I don't really watch TV anymore."

"Oh," she says, looking down.

"What about you?"

"My mom doesn't let me watch TV during the school year."

"Same here," I say, and immediately think of the telenovelas on until midnight in the living room, mama translating what the characters say into English, baba repeating it back to her in Arabic so she could hear how strong it sounded and how smooth

Spanish is by contrast, and him explaining how one cancels out the other. How neutral the two of them are together. How necessary.

I finish the last grape. “Do you want to play volleyball?”

Ana scans the ground for the nearest ball and points to one across the field. We run to it.

When the school day ends, mama's car pulls up to the front of the school, the brakes squeaking hard. The teacher up front asks her which kid she is here to pick up. Who does she nanny for?

She rolls down the window. "Huh?" mama says.

"Yes," the teacher says. "Uh, caregiver, babysitter." He looks for more words. Then he turns around, looks at the students waiting to be picked up. "Hey," he says, looking at me, "can you translate something for me?"

I stand up.

"Can you ask her which kid she is here to pick up?"

"So," mama says after a few minutes, after the principal's apology on behalf of the teacher, the teacher's own apology, after my classmates pointed, saying, "Look, it's the new girl," whispering, hushed. Mama adjusts the air conditioner, angles the vent toward herself. "How was it today?"

"I need a pencil case. And erasers and colored pencils and four notebooks," Rafa says, handing her a folded list from the back seat. "One of the notebooks has to be blue for math. And three of them have to be . . ." He pauses, flipping the paper over to check. "Spiraled." I look out the window as we pass the school parking lot, craning my head to see the students waiting to be picked up. Are they still whispering?

Mama takes Rafa's paper and sets it on her lap. "We'll work on it."

"Mr. Lewis says I need all of it by tomorrow."

"I get my next paycheck on Friday," she says, turning into a tunnel. It is too dark now to see either of their faces but I hear it in mama's voice, the frustration, the way she spaces out every word. "I'll write a note."

"A note? I need everything by tomorrow."

"Hey," she says. "Listen. I'll write him a note."

When he puts his list back in his backpack, his elbow knocks over the water bottle in the cup holder. All over my lap, streaming down my thighs. I pick it up. The bottle is half empty now, drenching my shoes. Water pools in the pads of my socks, between my toes.

"Rafa," I say, holding up the water bottle, shaking the water off my backpack. "Can't you be a little more careful?"

"Sofia," mama says.

"What? If it wasn't for his stupid elbow, we wouldn't be here right now." I turn to him. "Seriously, Rafa," I say. "What, spilling the orange juice wasn't enough? And we just got this water bottle, too. It was full." I screw on the lid and put it back in the cup holder.

"I didn't mean to," he says.

I cannot see his face in the dark, but I know what it looks like. He starts to cry. I can hear it, the sniffling, the short, short breaths.

Mama wants me to apologize. It was not Rafa's fault, she says. He is little. A little boy. "Say it."

"Fine. Sorry," I say, taking off my shoes, then my socks. I face my window. When we exit the tunnel, sunlight falls on us like sharp yellow leaves.

"We're dividing fractions today," Ms. Clyde tells us after morning prayer the next day. She tells us to settle in our seats. "I can wait," she says, tapping her foot. "Thank you." She writes today's date on the board in winding cursive and then sets down the marker. "We need all of Jesus's help for this," she says, laughing to herself. "Can someone remind me what a fraction is? Just a rough definition."

The room falls silent. Only the hum of the fish tank.

She taps her chin with her finger. "Do I need to start calling on people randomly?"

The boy to my right puts his head down on his desk. I raise my hand.

"Ana," she says, pointing at me with her marker.

"Sofia," I say.

"Yes. Sofia."

I use the example my teacher told us last year. "It's like how a slice of pizza is part of the entire pizza," I say. "When something is part of something else."

"Great, yes," she says. "Now, when it comes to dividing fractions, it's very helpful to know how to multiply fractions. Does anyone remember from last year how we multiply fractions? Do we multiply straight across, like this? Or do we multiply diagonally, like this?"

"Straight across," I say.

Ms. Clyde looks at me. "We only speak when we raise our hands."

"Oh," I say, looking around the room. "Sorry."

She stops in her tracks and shakes her head. "You did it again, honey. Class, remind me. We only speak . . ."

"When we raise our hands," the class echoes.

"But yes, that's right. We multiply straight across." She continues on.

"Show-off," someone whispers, barely loud enough for me to hear. No one else seems to have noticed, not even the boy to my right, tossing his eraser from one hand to the other.

Later, when Ms. Clyde asks what a reciprocal is and I know it, I look around the room. When no one else raises their hand, I raise mine, and she says, "Anyone else?"

I put my hand down. My stomach rumbles so loud, the girl sitting in front of me turns around, her curly blond hair flicking off her shoulder. A few minutes later, when it happens again and I want to disappear, she reaches into her backpack and grabs something—a shiny green granola bar—and sets it on my desk.

"Oh," I whisper when Ms. Clyde has her back turned to us. "Thank you."

"No problem," she says.

I doubt we are allowed to eat in class, so I slip it into my pocket. I want to ask if I could go to the restroom so I can eat it there, and I almost do, but I look at Ms. Clyde, at the way she twists the cap from the dry-erase marker like a head from a body, her fingers wrapped around the marker's throat. I sit back in my seat, interlace my hands on my desk, and wait for the bell to ring.

"You know, Ms. Clyde isn't as bad as she seems," Ana says at lunchtime, dipping a carrot into a small container of ranch then scraping the excess off the edge. "Sometimes, she gives a gift card to the person who gets the highest score on a quiz. Mr. Schubert never did that." She wipes the corner of her mouth with a napkin.

"Mr. Schubert?"

"The fifth-grade teacher," she says, reaching for her water bottle. I have to squint to see Ana. The sky is pure light, the sun reflecting off the metal benches. Birds perch on the electrical wires that hang over the playground, their yellow beaks stark against their black feathers. When they fly away, their wings flap loudly, the sound of someone shaking out a rug each time they take off. "Where's your lunch box?"

"I had a big breakfast," I say, and put my hand above my eyes to block out the sun. I take out the granola bar from my pocket. "What kind of gift card?"

Ana shrugs. "Changes every time. The first time, it was to a smoothie place. The second time . . ." She pauses. "I think it was to an ice cream shop."

"Have you gotten one?"

She shakes her head. "Ashley always gets it. Every time. But I usually get second place."

"Do you get something?"

"No. I wish," she says, biting into a carrot.

"Who's Ashley again?"

Ana points to a girl a few tables behind us, two dangly gold earrings hanging from her ears, her hair blond, curly, and long. "She's kind of a jerk, though. At least her dad is. They fire a new maid every week," she says, unzipping a plastic bag full of pretzels. "My cousin worked for them once. Said it was the worst job she ever had. And you know where she worked before that?"

"Where?"

"The dump."

I turn around and look over at Ashley again, but this time, she notices. She smiles at me. I smile back politely and then turn toward Ana. A cloud passes over the schoolyard, shading us. I can put my hand down. The cloud above us looks as round and fluffy as a scoop of vanilla ice cream.

Ana reaches into her plastic bag, takes out a handful of pretzels, places them on a napkin, and pushes it forward to me. "Why don't you take some?"

"Are you sure?"

"My dad packed me too many anyway."

On Thursday I get called into Ms. Monique's office.

"Hi, sweetie. Come right in," she says warmly, standing up from her chair to wave me into the room. A vase of violets sits near her computer, their heads arching toward the table as if in prayer. The window behind her desk opens up to a view of the parking lot, the white and gray cars lined up like teeth, each in their own slot. The room smells strongly of pumpkin pie, like one is baking here, browning, in the office. I follow the scent to an orange candle by the fax machine. "How are you?"

"Good and you?"

"Good, good. Listen, I have something I need you to give to your mom, okay?" She hands me a yellow sticky note with a name, phone number, and address written in slanted cursive. "Tell her he's expecting you all tonight. Unfortunately, it's just until Saturday morning because we have a long wait list full of people. But hopefully it helps."

I take the sticky note from her hand. "I'll tell her."

"I hope it works out for you three. I really do."

"Thank you." I look down at the note, the sticky part pressed against my index finger. She smiles at me, and I close the door gently behind me before walking back to my classroom.

Mr. Leonard has a wobble about him. He moves his legs slowly, balancing on them like they are about to snap. He looks about eighty or maybe older, his blue buttoned cardigan tucked into his pants and his glasses settled low on his nose, right above his nostrils.

He ushers us inside, saying, "Come in, come in. It's windy out. Nina, right?" he asks mama, and extends his hand.

"Yes," she says graciously. "And you're Mr. Leonard."

"Joseph," he says, and shakes her hand. "Let me show you around." He closes the front door, leading us through the living room to the rest of the house. The couch, brown and suede, is across from a TV fixed on a metal stand, a few feet away from a table cluttered with newspapers and coffee-ringed coasters. "It's a shame, really, that no one in my family gets much use of this house anymore. It's just me here. Grandkids come around during the holidays sometimes, but that's about it. So I thought, hey, why not open it up to people who need it?"

"That's very kind of you," mama says. I can tell by the way she is looking at his feet that she wants to ask if we should take off our shoes. But he keeps his shoes on and walks farther into the house, so we do too.

We follow him down a hallway, where picture frames cover most of the wall. There are babies wearing lace bonnets; women with big, loose curls holding diplomas at their chests; a tall man standing in a gazebo, smiling with his whole mouth, his hand to his cheek. Some of the pictures are matte in black and white, some in glossy color. The biggest picture is in the center of the wall, three or four times as large as the rest: a woman with gray hair that comes up to her ears, a silver cross around her neck. "That's my Rachel," he says when he notices me looking at it.

I look at mama, who nods.

"She's beautiful," I say, because I think that is what she would say. What she wants me to say, anyway.

"She really was," he says, reaching out to touch the edge of the photograph. "All right, so, bathroom's here. Bedroom there. Mine's over there, around the corner. And, well," he says, looking at the three of us, "make yourself at home. I usually sleep around nine, just so you know."

"Thank you so much," mama says. "Kids?"

"Thank you," Rafa and I say.

"It's nothing," he says, smiles, and turns toward his room. "Just glad I could help."

We set our bags by the bedroom door on the dark orange carpet. Looking around the room, I see a wooden headboard with rods pointing up like spears, a metal crucifix hanging by the doorframe. There are mirror closet doors that squeak when you roll them open, a tan dresser with matching bedside tables. A triangular cuckoo clock between the two large windows sticks out like a nose between two eyes.

"What's that?" Rafa asks, pointing to something on one of the bedside tables.

"That's a lava lamp. Never thought I'd see one of those again," mama says, picking it up and shaking it lightly before setting it back on the table. "We can plug it in before we go to bed. It's prettier in the dark."

Rafa showers first.

When he comes out of the bathroom, steam follows like someone waiting behind him. The way Rafa smells, it is as if he has transformed the room into a flower garden—a rosebush suddenly by the bed, sprouting from the carpet, the flowers dangling like pink bells.

Mama next. She grabs a towel from the bed and takes it with her into the bathroom. While she showers, I put my books on the bookshelves and start to fold my clothes to put into the dresser but then stop, bringing them up close to smell them. I put them down. Sour. Maybe we can do laundry here.

Fifteen minutes later, it is my turn.

I turn on the hot water, the steam already clouding up the glass shower door. The bathroom has sky-blue tiles, a white tub. I step inside and then glide it closed. I use the warm, sudsy sponge to make streaks of fluffy white bubbles on my legs, my arms, washing off the day, the car, letting it drain down, away. I hum, throwing my head back in the water. I wet my hair, work in the shampoo, then wash it out. The conditioner silkens the floor. I brush through my hair with my fingers, rinse off one last time, then turn the knob all the way to the right, cutting off the water.

That night, in the warm light of the chandelier hanging over the dining table, Mr. Leonard tells us a story about "the war," not specifying which one, and mama, Rafa, and I listen intently and politely until it is eight fifty-five and he rises from the table to get ready for bed.

"Sleep well," he tells us. His beard, thin and white, puffs out from underneath his bottom lip like a small cloud.

"Thank you."

"We will."

"You too."

And we do. There is no tossing, no turning. There is only us and the night and the lava lamp, casting a soft, shifting orange glow on the three of us, like a sunset is breathing.

Early next morning, before we leave for school, Mr. Leonard goes out for a long walk with his neighbor, a woman in a ribbed purple jacket who takes him by the arm, and it is almost like we own the place. Mama opens the three windows in the living room—windows so large they stretch from the floor to the ceiling. Daylight folds over itself like fresh sheets, warming the armrests on the couch. And outside, gold leaves shimmer on the trees like layers of necklaces. The trees are so close, just a few inches from the windows. I reach out to touch the bark, the roughness of it.

Mama brews coffee. Rafa flips on the TV and sits on the couch. I join him. Then when mama's coffee is ready—sweetened and creamed and stirred—so does she. She lands in a plop next to us. We watch cartoons, slightly grainy on the screen. We laugh at the characters. At their misfortune. Their slipping on a banana peel, their getting hit over the head with an anvil, their flattening under a dropped piano. We are relieved, I think, to be better off than some people.

After school, Mama washes and dries our clothes, then folds them while Rafa and I do our homework. Mr. Leonard orders a pizza for dinner, and later, when the plates are cleared, we all stack dominoes like bricks, building a house, the four of us holding our breath until it all crashes, then laughing when it finally does.

Saturday morning, mama tells us, yawning, to get our stuff together. It is time for the next people on the list to come and stay here. It is seven and they will be here at nine fifteen. Mama lifts a corner of the sheet off the bed and then tells me to grab a new set of sheets from the closet.

Rafa throws a fit.

"But I don't want to go," he says, pulling the blanket over his head. Then he starts to cry. Loud, wailing. I know what he is feeling—we just got here, just unpacked—but if Mr. Leonard sees him like this, or hears him, he will not want to have us back. Mama untucks another corner of the sheet.

"Hey," I say, pulling the blanket, damp now, off his head. "It's okay."

When we were driving back to Mr. Leonard's house after picking up the pizza last night, Rafa asked if we were stopping anywhere else before going home and mama snapped her head back at that word, "home," and said, "It's not *home* home, Rafa. Tomorrow's our last day there," and he could not believe it. "I just don't want you to get your feelings hurt, thinking we live there now," she said. I knew we would be leaving soon, but it still felt too fast. I had only unpacked my books the day before, had barely learned the layout of the house. Rafa shook his head the whole drive back to Mr. Leonard's house, saying, "No no no. No no no."

"Where to now?" I ask her, stuffing my clothes into my backpack. We know where. I look around the room, at the orange carpet beneath my feet, at the cuckoo clock ticking.

Rafa sits up and crosses his arms. "I'm not going."

"It's just temporary," she reassures us. "Get one more shower in, both of you."

When it is my turn to shower, after Rafa, I use double the amount of shampoo I used last time, scrubbing it deep into my scalp with my fingernails, to make it last twice as long.

While mama is packing up the rest of our clothes, folding our uniform shirts, stacking Rafa's pants, I walk into the living room, where Mr. Leonard is sitting at the dining table filling out the crossword puzzle, rubbing a gray eraser across the bottom corner of the newspaper.

"Mr. Leonard?" I say.

He looks up.

I think of what I should say, what it would take for him to let us stay here. I would keep the room clean, of course. I would keep the whole house clean, too, if he showed me where he kept the sprays and rags and mop. Not a smudge on the windows. The sinks, each one of them, sparkling white. I can cook. If he tells me what he likes, I can look up recipes at the library and make a list of ingredients. And Rafa, he would help. And mama, she is a nurse. That could be useful, given his age, his wobble. We could stay here. And it would be good for all of us.

I open my mouth to speak, then stop. It seems like he knows what I am thinking, the sudden face he makes, the way he looks down. He pushes his chair out a little and angles himself toward my direction.

"Hopefully Monique arranges for you all to come back soon," he says. "Besides, we need a rematch for those dominoes."

I breathe out. "That sounds nice," I say.

On the drive to the clinic afterward, while we are stopped at a red light, two teenagers cross the street wearing neon orange jackets. It is the same orange as the Nerf guns Lena, Chloe, and I played with for hours last summer, chasing each other through the long hallways at Chloe's beach house, crouching down, hiding in pillow forts, taking cover under the plush plum cushions. We called it Training. We Trained for hours. We came up with the idea when, at dinner one night, Chloe's mom said something about how the world does not like little girls, or likes them too much, and how either situation is a worst-case scenario. That we would have to be prepared when we were older.

After dinner that day, we dug through Chloe's older brother's closet and grabbed handfuls of foam darts, shoving them deep into our pockets. We aimed at empty water bottles, at trash bags we stuffed with old newspapers and shaped into men, which slumped over when we hit them. We named all of them Jeffrey, after Chloe's dad, who left when she was a baby. We kept score. We all won, we decided, drinking hot chocolate after, the marshmallows dissolving like cotton balls. We were ready.

After the two boys finish crossing the street, I try thinking of anything besides Chloe and Lena: sand fleas, wind, pink elephants. The pink elephants work until I remember that Lena's favorite color is pink. I lean my head against the window, trying to think of purple elephants—purple trunks and tails and toes. Chloe's favorite color is blue, so there should be no problem.

It works for a minute.

Mama must have parked underneath a sapping tree without knowing it. I wake up early on Sunday morning to a buzzing sound so loud, it must be right by my ear, whatever it is, sitting on my earlobe. My eyes blink open. A bee lands on Rafa's shoulder, its wings thin and crinkly like plastic wrap pressed against itself.

I swat it off him.

It lands on the window closest to me, nibbling on something yellow dripping down the glass and onto the armrest. I reach my hand out to touch it. It feels thick. Something like maple syrup, sticky, hardened. When I turn toward the front of the car to look for a napkin, I see that the windshield is covered in bugs—bees, wasps, ladybugs. Flies with bodies as big as blackberries. Hundreds of crawling legs. I see squirrels licking the windshield wipers, their bushy paintbrush tails pointed up in the air. I shriek when I feel something land on the bridge of my nose, near the corner of my eye, and see two thin brown antennae wiggling against my eyelashes. Mama wakes up, then Rafa.

We open the doors and tumble out of the car, running away from it. Mama tells us to cover our noses so that the bugs do not get inside.

"What about our ears?" Rafa asks, his voice muffled, his hand cupped over his nose.

"Those too," she says.

"I don't have that many hands," I say.

The sky is still dark, stained purple-blue, practically night—too early for a car wash to be open. Looking at mama panting, I can tell she is trying to come up with a plan. Her eyebrows are knit tight, focused.

"Chloe's beach house has a hose in the front yard," I say. "They go there on the weekends. It's nearby, right?"

Mama glances over at me, thinking.

"Today's Sunday. They might be there," I say.

She nods, then reaches into her pocket for her phone. "Damn it," she says. "I left it in the cup holder."

Together, on the count of three, we pinch our noses and rush to the car. We get in as fast as we can, slamming the doors the second we get inside, rolling the windows up all the way. Only one bug is left inside, a harmless ant.

She says she wants to wait an hour or two before calling Sue, Chloe's mom, to give her a chance to wake up. But really, I know mama cannot stand Sue. Last year, when she gave me and Lena laptops for Christmas, mama made me return mine. "It's like she's trying to prove a point. We get it, she's swimming in money," she said then. Now mama says she will try something else first so that we might not even need to call her. I know I should not, but I cross my fingers and hope whatever it is does not work. It has been weeks since I last saw Chloe.

"Ready?" she says.

Mama tells us to brace ourselves. She steps on the gas, driving fast so the wind blows the bugs away from the car. It works while we are driving but when we reach a red light the bugs surround the car again, looming around us like a buzzing multicolored cloud.

"Okay, then." She pulls into a parking spot and lets out a long sigh, blinks, and picks up her phone.

"Hey, Sue, how are you? Sorry, I know it's early, but listen, we're by the beach and we were wondering," she says, pausing when Sue interrupts. I look at the dashboard. It is seven in the morning. "Yes, definitely. Sofia will be thrilled." Mama puts on her "proper" voice around parents from school, using words like "definitely" and "absolutely" and "surely." I look at her weirdly when she does this, part of me wondering if I should be doing the same.

"Excellent," she says into the phone. "Thank you." She hangs up. Breathes out.

When we get there the sky is still dark. The lamppost in front of Sue's house throws orange light on the sidewalk, like someone dropped a can of paint there, by the driveway. All of our stuff, our clothes, our backpacks, our plastic spoons, it is all in the trunk. Mama told us to put it there before we drove here so Sue, "snoopy Sue," mama calls her, would not ask any questions. "Or worse," mama said on the drive over, "get the wrong idea."

Mama turns off the car, the front door of the house swings open, and Chloe appears at Sue's side still in her pajamas, a black nightgown with white sailboats and anchors, before running up to the car and hugging me. I hug her back. Her hair smells like caramel, like molasses. When mama explains about the bugs, Sue unravels a long green hose behind a bush and brings us a bottle of dish soap and pack of sponges from the kitchen.

The five of us take turns spraying down the car, scrubbing, then spraying until our clothes are drenched, dark and heavy with water. A large puddle forms around the car. A mosquito stops above it, hovering over its own reflection. Its legs, thin twigs breaking the surface tension. I swat it away.

Thirty minutes later, when the sun has come up and the car is scrubbed clean, Sue asks us if we want to stay for breakfast.

I answer before mama can say no. “We’d love to.”

“Yes, that would be lovely,” mama says.

When Sue turns to walk into the house, mama gives me a look. I shrug it off. I look up. Above us, a yolk sun breaks through egg-white clouds.

In the sunrise Chloe's house looks like a stone castle.

Palm trees arch over the front porch, their husked heads bowing down to the iron door. And there it is: the silver doorknob that annoys mama even more than Sue does. Last summer, Sue hired a painter to brush it bronze for "an aged look," flying him in from Italy for twenty minutes' worth of work. Mama scoffed at that, saying the doorknob would have tarnished in its own time. "What some people do with their money," she said.

"Come in, come in," Sue says, singsongy, placing her keys on the kitchen counter. We slip off our wet shoes and leave them by the welcome mat.

Inside, a painting of the coast takes up an entire wall, the blue shoreline shimmering along the sand, a pelican with orange legs squatting on a fence. When we were here last, mama whispered to me, genuinely confused, saying she did not understand the point of this painting, that Sue could simply pull back the curtains and look outside and there, right there, would be the same exact view.

In the dining room, a chandelier that looks like a gold crown with teal jewels sways above the dining table, the breeze jingling the jewels. A delicate wind-chime song.

Mama helps Sue make breakfast, pulling a carton of eggs from the fridge, setting a jug of orange juice on the counter.

"You girls go have fun," Sue says. "We'll let you know when breakfast is ready."

After Rafa dries off, wringing out his shirt over the sink in the bathroom, he stays to help, reaching for a mixing bowl. Sue rummages through a low drawer and hands mama and Rafa aprons, then wraps one around herself.

"So," Chloe says, drying off with a towel in her room, "why'd you leave? You could've told us you were leaving." She hands me the towel, damp and weighted.

I take it from her and dry off my arms, my neck. "It's not like I knew I was leaving." It comes out more defensive than I would like, so I clear my throat. "It was a last-minute thing." I borrow mama's phrase. "A family emergency."

"Whatever you say," she says, running a large red comb through her hair. "You missed my birthday, you know."

"I know."

"No card or anything. No phone call."

"I know. I'm sorry."

"No present."

I think about my backpack in the trunk, what I could pull out to give her. My library book, maybe. But then I think of the bookshelves downstairs in the living room, so tall, Sue had a ladder installed to reach the highest shelf. They probably own a copy of the book. And anyway, Chloe does not like to read.

After she finishes brushing her hair, we sit cross-legged by the foot of her bed, a knit blanket draped over our knees. She plays with the tassels, braiding the individual strings. She tells me her family is going to Norway for Christmas, that she got a Polaroid camera for her birthday and is looking forward to taking pictures of the snowy mountains, the northern lights glowing above them, electric green and neon pink and deep blue. "What are you doing for Christmas?"

I pick at the threads of the blanket. "I'm not sure yet."

"You're acting all quiet. Like, really quiet," she says. I open my mouth to speak, but she cuts me off. "Oh!" she says, lighting up. "Did you hear about Ms. McCoy and Mr. Scout?"

I shake my head. "No, I didn't. Wait. Are they—"

"You called it. They're getting married."

"No way," I say, and I try to act excited, even if I am distracted. Part of me is trying to figure out a way to stay here, with Chloe and Sue. Maybe if I told them we were living in our car, they would take us in. Rafa and I could go back to our old school. It would be easy. We could carpool.

I try to sort out the details at breakfast, looking down at my plate, at the fluffy scrambled eggs and jam-slathered toast and full glass of milk I could be having every day if I asked. I take a sip of milk, looking over at mama, who is indulging Sue by asking a follow-up question about her investments, leaning in to appear interested. I know she would be furious if I said anything about staying. I can see it now: her face red, twisted. "Just. Leave. Things. Alone," she would say, digging her nails into my arm. I tip the glass upward, finishing the milk. I pour myself another glass and then reach across the table for another slice of toast.

When we say goodbye, I take a long look at the house: at the wide, shiny open windows, the leaves rusting red-brown on the oak tree outside, the one whose branches we climbed in the summer.

I hug Chloe goodbye, then Sue. The way Chloe looks down at my hands after we pull away, I can tell she expects me to give her a present, that she thinks I must have been hiding one this whole time to surprise her. Mama says we will see them soon and I wave goodbye, hands empty.

We attend the Spanish Mass at seven thirty at night. As quietly as we can, we push through the heavy doors and walk into the church, the turquoise light floating down, down from the stained-glass windows and landing on the back of our heads, our shoulders, like we are at the bottom of a swimming pool. Father Cervantes, much older than Father Charles, with a gray mustache above his purply lips, officiated last week. The week before, it was Father Garcia, who cleared his throat every few seconds while delivering the sermon.

Rafa did not understand anything Father Cervantes or Father Garcia said. I followed along through most of it, but last week, toward the end, a woman in a floral dress bent down, held up the book of hymns, and asked me, in Spanish, what page we were on. I could not remember how to say "256," so I tugged on mama's shoulder and had her help instead. At times like this I wish I were wearing a shirt that said "I understand Spanish but can't really speak it well," something I could point to without having to explain. Maybe the back of the shirt would say "I'm sorry."

"Finally," Rafa said after the service ended and people gathered outside. There was candle smoke in our hair, incense in our clothing. "Do we have to do this every week?"

"Every week," mama said, so here we are.

But tonight, it is seven forty-five, and Mass still has not started. Mama looks down at her watch. A few minutes later, a priest steps out, apologizes, and says, out of breath, in patchy Spanish, worse than mine, that Father Cervantes called in sick at the last minute and that he hopes the congregation can pray for him tonight. The priest turns to face the crowd. Father Charles. Mama breathes in sharply. He asks us all to stand. We do. Twenty minutes later, in the commotion of Communion, we move to a pew at the very back of the church. As soon as the service ends, mama has us slip out through the side door.

We never go back.

At recess on Monday, Cindy, the smallest girl in our class, pulls a bag of cherries out of her lunch box and empties it on the table, the cherries tumbling out hard like rubies, dark and gleaming. She swats the boys away. "Shoo. Shoo!" she says, then turns to face us, pushing her hair behind her ears. "Girls only." But the boys still watch, planted like trees a few feet away, shading us.

"Don't worry, I already washed them," she says.

Ashley leans close to the table. "Are they—"

"Yes, Ashley, they're organic."

I look at Ana, who shrugs. After morning prayer, Cindy had handed notes to all of the girls in class telling us to sit together at recess. Ana and I already planned on playing four square with the seventh graders, but we decided lunchtime four square was no different from four square at recess, minus the shade.

Cindy tells each of us to take a cherry. I place one in my palm. She tells us to tie the stem into a knot, and Ashley, sitting to my left, starts with her fingers.

"No, no, not with your hands," Cindy says. "With your tongue."

"Oh," says Ashley, setting the cherry down on the table. "Why?"

Cindy tells us that this is how to kiss. Her cousin, a freshman in high school, learned it from a TV show Cindy was not allowed to watch. If you kiss like this, your husband will never leave you, her cousin said, and then I think of mama, then baba, and I put the cherry down even though I am hungry.

Ashley's face flushes. Almost as red as the cherry.

"What are we doing over here, ladies?" Mr. Lewis walks over and says, holding a clipboard close to his chest.

"Sharing snacks," Cindy says. "Want one?" She offers the bag to him, dangling it in the air.

The teacher looks at us suspiciously. "Sure," he says, squinting. He reaches into the bag and takes one. When he leaves, we all laugh.

Then when he is out of sight, something falls onto the table from up high—a stem tied into a knot—and I look up to see who dropped it: a boy our age, maybe a year or two older, with straight black hair. Ana blushes. Shrinks.

"Gross, Antonio," Cindy says, whining, flicking it off the table and then rubbing her hands on her skirt. "That was in your *mouth*."

While the rest of the girls make fake throw-up noises, clutching their throats, Ana looks around, finds the cherry stem on the ground, and slips it into her pocket. I raise my eyebrow.

"What?" she says.

I turn around. The boy does, too, a few feet away now. Antonio. He smiles at me, his hair sweeping across his forehead. I smile back.

Ms. Clyde tells us to get ready for art class, opening the storage closet and pulling a tub labeled "Colors" down from a high shelf. Our desks cleared, she walks around the room and hands each of us a pack of pastels. We get to choose: oil or chalk. I want to ask if I can use paint instead, even finger paint will do, but I do not see any in the tub.

"Oil or chalk?" she asks me.

"Oil," I say. "Thank you."

A few months ago, when I asked baba why he never painted for fun anymore, like he used to, he said it was because he did not have time. I asked him if he missed it. "Of course," he said. "Why wouldn't I?" Once, when I was younger, he set up two wooden easels side by side, one for me and one for him, twenty or so open bottles of paint surrounding us like potions. Squeezed-out tubes of white, tubs of primer, jars of paint thinner. A handful of brushes in a cup of cloudy water. He unwrapped canvases for both of us, the plastic wrap shimmering down to the floor, and said he would paint a sunset if I painted a sunrise. After we finished, he took the thinnest brush he had and added birds to both of our paintings, adding black crows to his, white doves to mine, up by the clouds.

I look down at my pastels. He must have more time to paint

now. Maybe after work he unfolds the blue tarp and sets it on the garage floor. Maybe he locks the wooden easel into place, chooses a canvas. He picks up a brush. But what does he paint? Or who? Who does he paint?

Just as Ms. Clyde sets a blue vase of sunflowers on the stool in front of the whiteboard for us to draw, a shadow passes over the window at the top of our classroom door, blocking the light that passes through. We all look up. Someone is looking in, wearing a black shirt and pants, a white collar around his neck. Ms. Clyde walks over from her podium, her flats clacking against the carpet as she walks toward the door, then opens it.

"Can we help you, Father?"

"No, no," he says, putting his hands in his pockets. "Just doing the rounds before school Mass."

"Of course." She swivels toward us. "Class, can we say good morning to Father Charles?"

It takes me a second to realize that everyone is standing up. I stand up, too, a second late.

"Good morning, Father Charles," the class says.

He gives a hearty, nervous laugh and steps into the classroom. "Well, good morning, sixth grade."

"Thanks for stopping by, Father," Ms. Clyde says, adjusting the flowers in the vase.

Something passes over his eyes. "You know what, actually," he says, turning to Ms. Clyde, whispering to her. "I wanted to see if I could speak to Sofia. You know, see how she's settling in."

My classmates turn to look at me.

"Oh," she says, putting her hands on her hips. "Well, that's very kind of you." She calls my name and waves me over. "Father wants to speak to you for a second."

He holds the door open and motions for me to walk outside, into the hallway. The door shut, I look through the window and make eye contact with about half of my classmates while Ms. Clyde passes out sheets of construction paper. Ana, sitting in the front row, cranes her neck to see.

Father Charles clears his throat. "I just want to see how you and your brother are settling in."

I nod. "Everyone's nice so far."

"Anyone giving you any trouble?"

"Trouble?" I say. "No."

"That's good. You know, your mom," he says, looking over his shoulder. "I don't know if she's—you know, if she," he starts to say, then stops and sighs, looking at me.

I wait for him to finish. "My mom?"

"Never mind." He lets out a deep breath and plasters a smile on his face. "I'm glad things are going well," he says, adjusts his collar, and starts to walk away, his left hand in his pocket, his right hand swinging by his side.

Later, at school Mass, I get in line for Communion behind Ana, and when I reach the front, I give Father Charles a polite smile. He frowns and places the wafer in my palm.

Next Thursday I have a test on ocean divisions. Ms. Clyde announced it in class before letting us out for recess. "A gift card," she said, standing in front of the whiteboard, "for the person with the highest grade."

After school I make flash cards by tearing sheets of white paper from the library into small squares, folding each sheet of paper in half and then in half again, before ripping it along the folds. I write the terms on one side of the flash cards and the definitions on the other—"seamount," "abyssal plane," "mid-ocean ridge," "bathyal zone," "continental shelf." Mama tests me on them every day after school. Sometimes, when we have already gone through them a few times and we have both begun to yawn, nodding off, mama will choose a word to intentionally mispronounce. "For fun," she says. "I can be funny, you know."

Tonight "beach" becomes "bitch." Mama, looking up from the index card all mischievous, eyes full of rare light, her brown hair slightly yellowed beneath the overhead, asks me in between which two ocean divisions we find the "bitch." She has already begun to laugh, her hand covering her mouth. I start to laugh, too, at the way she cracks herself up, laughing at something right after she says it, like she is her own audience.

"Between the coastal plain and the continental shelf," she says, "or between the continental shelf and the shelf break?"

"The first one."

"Say the full thing."

"The beach is between—"

She puts her hand up. "Nope."

I groan, smiling. "The bitch is between the coastal plane and the continental shelf."

"That's right. Now," she says, holding up the diagram I drew in class, "point to the bitch."

An hour later mama pulls out of the parking lot. After we finished studying, a police car parked a few stalls away from us, flashing red-blue-red-blue, so now we have to find a new place to park. She gets on the highway. We drive past racoons and possums lying along the railing, some curled up into balls of fur, others bloody, laid out like stained rugs. To my right, a raccoon's striped tail flaps around in the wind like a flag, its body flattened on the road, a black tire track down the middle.

Mama says the animals are sleeping. Tells us it is nighttime and animals have bedtimes too. Rafa almost believes her. We are driving too fast to get a closer look. But fifteen minutes later, when an accident up ahead slows the traffic down to a stop, Rafa points outside his window and tells us to look.

"There," he says, pressing his hands to the glass. "See?"

I look at Rafa's eyes first, wide and dark, and follow them out through the open window. Two small spotted fawns stoop down to a larger deer, one licking a red smudge on the deer's side, the other nudging around the wound with its black nub of a nose. The big deer does not move. Its legs stick out like stiff branches. I look at its belly, waiting for it to puff up with air, and for a second, I think it is breathing, but it is just the wind dizzying the fur. A cloud of flies glooms over the deer's belly and settles around both fawns, which shake them away with their ears.

"I know it's not sleeping," Rafa says. "You don't need to lie."

One of the fawns digs its small hooves into the big deer's side, like it is trying to get it to roll over.

"It is sleeping," mama says.

"There's red," he says.

"From eating cranberries."

"I don't see any cranberries."

The car lurches forward. Rafa turns back, but I tell him to look, look up ahead, there is a billboard for that superhero movie he has been wanting to see, the one with the three men holding shields. If he had looked back, he would have seen a pile of intestines, like fat pink worms tangled together, spilling out of the deer, steam rising up. He would have seen the two fawns lying down next to it, curled up right by its head, sniffing around her eyes, licking the space between them with small red tongues.

When mama pulls up at the gas station and tells us to stretch our legs and use the bathroom before we go to bed, I look both ways before getting out of the car.

"Come on." She motions with her hand for me to come join them. I place my feet on the ground, wobbly because I cannot get it out of my head, what I saw, and what I might see in the candy aisle of the gas station, the red licorice sticks, the gummy worms, the rolls of bubble gum tape, all of them, spilling out of the deer.

"Actually, I'm good," I say, and get back in the car. I watch as they walk into the white light of the gas station.

When Rafa gets in trouble for calling a girl a bitch during recess the next day, his teacher sends a note home. They were playing basketball. The girl, a fourth grader, would not pass the ball to him.

"Please advise your son," it says in red ink toward the bottom of the page, above the teacher's signature. Mama laughs. She fans herself with the note before tearing it in half.

I wipe the sweat off my forehead and notice that the small of my back is damp too. Heat melts its way through the windows and into the car, my elbows sticking to the armrests. I peel myself off the seat. "Isn't it December?" I say. "Why is it so hot?"

"I don't know, mija."

The heat makes us prickly. A few months ago, when the air-conditioning at the house broke, the four of us, short-tempered and overheated, would fight about the smallest things: the way the forks were organized in the utensil drawer, all crooked when it was so easy to line them up the right way; the useless little drink of milk left in the carton; the plants that wilted by the window because us damn kids had forgotten to water them. The stale breeze that drifted in through the windows made it worse, a warm exhale on my skin. Baba asked mama to stop wearing sleeveless shirts, saying he preferred her covered up when we were around other people, and she glanced around the living room and said, "What other people?" She looked at him in his white tank top and told him to cover up too. He refused, saying no one was looking at his chest. He made her bring a jacket wherever she went even though she never put it on.

"Here," she says, handing the two ripped halves of the teacher's note to me. "Two new index cards. For your test." She looks at Rafa. "Don't do that again, okay? People don't like it. It's not a nice word."

"But you said it," he says.

"I know, because I'm a grown-up."

"And Sofia said it."

"Sofia's older than you. And she said it because I told her to. Because we were joking."

"But I was joking too."

"Just listen to me, okay? Never again. No buts."

I can tell what he is about to do. All the warning signs are there, flashing red around his face. He tilts his chin up, looks right at her when he says it. "Bitch."

A flash of hurt crosses her eyes so briefly that I wonder if I could have imagined it. She pinches his wrist with her fingernails. "Hey," she says. "You never, ever say that again, you understand me?" She pinches harder, and he winces. "You got it?"

"Okay, okay," he says, whining, rubbing his wrist.

Sometimes, when baba helped me with math homework, mama would brew tea in a shiny porcelain pot, the dried mint at the bottom swirling around the tea leaves. Baba and I sat at the dining table with my worksheets on top, so many of them, it was like we had spread a white tablecloth over the wooden table, dirtied with pencil scribbles and pen marks.

He whispered to himself, counting in Arabic. When he mumbled, his eyes would move up and down like he was looking at a chalkboard. He tried teaching me the way he was taught in Egypt—dividing down like this, multiplying like that, tricks that made the math faster, easier. But when I got points deducted on a quiz for using his shortcuts, he took it personally. In Mr. Scout's red pen at the top of the page: "We didn't learn this in class." And once: "No cheating." One time, I got fifteen points off. "This is the way I know," baba said when I showed him the quiz. "The way I was taught. Why would they have you use the slow way? The stupid way?"

"I don't know, baba."

He sighed. "Okay," he said, drawing a line down the middle

of a blank piece of paper. "On the left, you do it my way. On the right, you do," he said, pausing, then shaking his head. "Whatever this is. Your teacher's way." He placed the paper in front of me. "Start from the beginning."

"The beginning of what?"

"This," he said, picking up my quiz, waving it.

"The whole quiz?"

When baba got angry it happened in stages. First he scooted his seat closer to the table, started tapping his heel against the floor. If I made another mistake—he especially hated if my sevens did not have a line through the middle, saying the difference between one and seven is that line—he spoke extra slowly, straining each syllable. Then, after that, he might slam his palm on the table, or on his thigh, and it would feel like a small earthquake, the pens rattling off the edge of the table. I could feel the reverberations in my toes. The last stage was confusing because it was when he would call me "habibi." As if he was reminding himself who I was, his daughter.

"Yes, habibi. The whole thing." And he said it through his teeth.

That night, I had a whole presentation to outline, two chapters of a book to read, three discussion questions to answer, a worksheet to review for a history practice quiz, and on top of that, the new issue of *National Geographic* had just arrived in the mail, plastic-wrapped, waiting on the desk in my bedroom. "I don't have time," I said quietly.

"What?"

"I don't have time."

He reached forward so fast I thought he was going to hit me, so I closed my eyes and shielded my face. But he grabbed my wrist, put a pencil in my hand, and guided it to the table.

"Start from the top."

His foot, tapping.

At school the next day, in whispers during drop-off, there is talk of an eighth grader named Lisa and her mom's breast cancer. It is a bag of words mixed up and thrown in the air, settling around us like ash, words like "remission" and "terminal" and "spread." It is cold enough that we can actually see the whispers, little puffs of white from parents' lips in the morning cold.

During morning prayer, when we pray for the sick, I notice people bending forward to glance at her, even teachers. She does not seem to notice. Her head is low, a small pink ribbon pinned to her collar.

"So, I've heard some things," Ana says, sitting down at the table for lunch, unzipping her lunch box. The girls next to us are holding up their fingers, comparing the moods on their mood rings. Riley is blue and Calm. Cindy, purple and In Love. Rumor has it that because Lisa's mom cannot do her own makeup anymore, her dad learned how to do it for her by watching tutorials online, Ana says. I have only seen him once, during pickup—he wore a blue-and-green plaid vest and people called him "Doctor" even though he does not work at a hospital—but I can picture him with an eye shadow palette and a makeup brush. A pink cloud of blush blooming around the two of them as he applies it to her cheeks.

"I doubt it's true," Ana says, biting into her apple.

"How come?"

"Because that's not how men work," she says. "Like, my dad is great, but he'd never do that." She takes another bite of her apple, carving a white hole into the red skin, covering her mouth as she chews.

Riley and Cindy slide their mood rings to us from across the table. "I don't want to," Ana says, sliding them back, but Cindy scoots closer, grabs Ana's hand, and slips it on. It turns purple after a few seconds. "Oh," Cindy says, bringing her face close to the ring. "Ana's in love."

"With who?" Riley says. "We won't tell."

Ana gets up. "I'm not." She takes off the ring, throws it on the table, and walks toward the water fountain. The ring lands in between Riley's shoes. Two teachers, Mrs. Gonzales and Mrs. Donovan, hear it fall and look in our direction and then shrug, as if deciding not to investigate. I frown at Riley and Cindy for making her wear the ring, at Ana for almost causing a scene.

"What's with her?" Riley says, bending down to pick it up.

Cindy shrugs. "Who knows."

They both turn to me. "Do you want to try?"

"No thanks."

I look toward the water fountain, where Ana is standing, facing me. She is tapping her foot like she is waiting for me to follow. I push myself off the bench and walk over.

After school we park in a department store parking lot, facing a purple sunset, blackbirds swooping down into the trees. The leaves rustle. Mama sets her keys in the cup holder.

"If you were dying of cancer and couldn't do your makeup anymore, do you think baba would have done it for you?" I ask, then put my hands up by my face. "I mean, before all this. When things were good."

She tilts her head at me, confused. "What?"

"Because at school," I say, suddenly embarrassed at the question when I said it out loud. "Never mind." I already know the answer. I cannot imagine baba holding a tube of mascara let alone watching a video to learn how to use it. "Let's just study."

"It's tomorrow, right? The test," mama says.

I nod, unzipping my backpack and pulling out the index cards, held together by a rubber band I took from Ms. Clyde's desk a few days ago when she was not looking.

"Thank goodness. You know, I think everything you learn in school is important in some way or another. But this," she says, pointing to the flash cards, "mija, never in my adult life have I ever used the phrase 'hadalpelagic zone.' Not once."

"Well, maybe I will," I say, sliding the rubber band off the stack of index cards. "Okay, let's start from the top."

"Oh, look," mama says, and holds up her finger, where a small eyelash, like a dark fingernail clipping, has stuck to it. She places it in my palm. "Make a wish."

I open the window and blow it out. A breeze carries it forward, forward, into the dark.

"All right, time's up," Ms. Clyde says, tapping her watch. "Pencils down."

I turn my Scantron face down, brushing the pink eraser shavings off the edge of the desk. They look like bits of cotton candy on the floor. I imagine an ant taking a piece of it all the way back to its colony only to find out it is rubber. Ana, up a few rows, blows air out of her mouth and then rests her head down on her desk. Ms. Clyde tells us to pass our papers forward.

"Remember?" she tells us, waving the Scantrons in her hand like a fan once she has collected them all, shifting her hair back. "There's a gift card up for grabs," she says, sitting on top of her desk now, ankles crossed. "Same deal. It will go to the person with the highest score."

I set my pencil next to my eraser. The test seemed easy enough. Of the thirty questions, there were only one or two that I felt unsure about, but mama says when that happens you have to go with your gut, and I did. I cross my fingers under my desk. I mouth the word to myself, "Please," imagining what it would be like to show up to the car with a gift card in hand, how proud mama would be, and maybe she would even tear up holding it, she would be that proud. A light bulb a row ahead of me is giving out, pulsing its yellow heartbeat. I place my hand on my chest. I feel it.

"What did you think of the quiz?" Ana asks me at lunch.

"I thought it was okay. My mom helped me study for it," I say, pulling a lunch ticket out of my pocket. Earlier today, Ms. Monique handed me a pack of lunch passes in an envelope, saying they should last me and Rafa a few weeks. She said they could not guarantee they could do it again after we run out, but she would try. "If you still need it by then, of course," she said.

Today's menu is a slice of pizza, pepperoni or cheese, a carton of milk, regular or chocolate, and peaches.

"I'll be right back," I say to Ana. "Going to get my lunch."

When I get to the front of the line, Mari, the chef, smiles as I approach with my tray. She sets a slice of pizza on a dark blue plate, strings of cheese stretching across it, then plops a mushy scoop of canned peaches next to the slice. She sets the plate on my tray. I breathe in the warmth, the yeasty smell of the dough, the garlic in the tomato sauce. Mari became mama's friend when she got lost trying to find the principal's office last week. A security guard had approached mama with a hand on the Taser clipped to his belt and asked her why she did not go through the metal detectors like she was supposed to, and when mama said she did not know she had to, he began to raise his voice and reach for his walkie-talkie with his other hand. Mari stepped between them. "She's new," she said, putting her hand up. "It's okay."

"Menso," Mari said when the security guard was not in earshot. Mama said they laughed and got to talking. Yesterday, Mari brought a jar of salsa wrapped in foil to give to mama. We bought a bag of chips from the market and had that for dinner. Just as I am about to lift my tray off the counter Mari reaches into her pocket and places three strawberry bonbons onto my plate. "¿Quieres?" she says with a wink.

"Gracias," I say, smiling.

After lunch, Ms. Clyde tells us all to settle down, that she could easily decide not to award a gift card this time if we cannot control ourselves, it is as simple as that. The light chatter turns to silence. "Okay, that's better."

"And the gift card goes to," she says, pausing for dramatic effect. Her words hang in the air, suspended. "What, no drumroll?"

The class drums their hands on their desks. I feel my heart thumping in my neck, crawling up to my ears.

"Sofia," she says.

The room relaxes, the people in the front turning back to look at me. "Here you go, honey."

"Thank you." I stand up to take it from her.

"I knew it," Ana says. She walks from the front of the room to the back to hug me while the rest of the class claps, the chatter resuming in the background like someone turning up the volume on a TV. Ashley, sitting in front of me, is clapping, too, her curly hair swinging off her chair as she turns to face me.

I smile and look down at the gift card in my hands. It is for fifteen dollars. A bakery a few blocks away. I remember the bakery because one day, when we parked behind it, I woke up to the smell of blueberry muffins so strong it was like I was in the oven with them. I can see it now as Ms. Clyde tells us to take out our history books: the chocolate-dipped scones, muffins with brown sugar streusel spilling over the wrapper, fruit tarts with strawberries cut into roses. Rafa would get a sprinkle doughnut, mama coffee and a red velvet cupcake with a swirl of cream cheese frosting on top, and me, I would get one of everything.

Ana and I are sitting outside on the grass after school waiting to be picked up, our ankles tucked beneath us, the straps of our shoes undone. The kindergarten teacher is shushing her students as the last of them file out of the building. When they are all lined up, they sing the goodbye song, holding hands. "Until tomorrow, tomorrow . . ." they sing.

When Ana is sure no one is looking, she nudges me with her elbow. She flashes her test at me, a large red *C-* on top of the page, before shoving it deep into her backpack. She says her dad is going to kill her.

"Don't be surprised if I don't come back tomorrow," she says. "Visit my gravestone, though. I like yellow roses."

"Maybe we can study together for the next one," I say without thinking it through. I want to take it back in case she asks to come over. "At lunch or something," I add.

"Okay, cool," she says, standing up, dusting off her skirt. I look to my right and see a silver car pulling up to the front of the school. Ana swings her backpack over her shoulder and asks me to wish her luck.

"Good luck."

"Remember. Yellow roses," she says.

"Yellow roses." I nod.

After they drive off, I move to the metal bench in front of the planter box and look up at the sky, at the clouds drifting in a blue soup. Mama said she might be a few minutes late today. She has an all-staff meeting at the clinic this afternoon. I scan the front of the school, looking for Rafa, who I find sitting with the third-grade boys, making faces at the third-grade girls when they have their backs turned to them, then laughing. Someone taps me on my shoulder.

"Sofia?"

I turn around. "Oh, hi, Ashley."

She is holding a folded piece of paper by her side. "I was wondering if you knew the answer to number nineteen on the test. I could've sworn it was A."

"Let me check." I pull my folder out of my backpack and skim down the quiz until I find number nineteen. "I put B. Fracture zone."

"Fracture zone, okay. Thank you," she says, circling it on her quiz. "Hey, you know, you should come over sometime. Maybe tomorrow? After school?"

"Oh," I say. "I mean, I'd need to ask my mom."

"Great! My dad will call your parents," she says, zipping up her backpack. "He's here." She bends down to gather her things and runs over to a sleek, almost slippery-looking white car, like one I might find taking up a full-page ad in a magazine, so new that not even sunlight had touched it yet. "See you tomorrow," she yells as she gets in the car.

I wait until Rafa is asleep to tell mama about the gift card, convinced that if I told her while he was awake, he would insist we drive straight to the bakery and would maybe cry until we did. I am not sure I want to use it yet. Mama puts her hands in the air when I show it to her.

"No way!" she whispers.

She reaches back to hug me, holds me so close I can smell the lemon from the hand sanitizer she used to wash her face before bed.

I tell her I want to wait to use it. "To have something to look forward to," I say, thinking about how, even if I only waited until tomorrow to use it, I could think about it for the whole day at school, imagining the almond croissants, the raspberry-topped cupcakes, and be happy, knowing what waited after the bell rang. I could spend days like this. Thinking about it. Full on the feeling.

"Whatever you want," she says. "It's yours, mija. You earned it." She holds it in her hands. "God, I wish my teachers paid me to learn when I was in school. Must be nice," she says, winking. I slip the gift card into my pocket.

"Hey, Sofia, I was wondering," Ashley starts to say when the lunch bell rings the next day, standing at my desk with her jacket folded over her arm. I slip my math textbook into my backpack. "Do you want to have lunch together?"

I look over at Ana a few rows up, close enough to have heard. She is fitting a new rack of staples into her mini polka-dot stapler, the hinge squeaking as she clamps it shut. She responds before I do.

"We usually eat outside," Ana says, putting the stapler into her pencil case then zipping it closed. "To get some sun."

Ashley hesitates. "I don't want to get too dark," she says. When Ana's face sharpens, she corrects herself. "I mean, the sun's bad for you, you know. It's probably poison."

I set my backpack on top of my chair.

"Unless," Ashley says, and looks down at her arms, pale, freckled. "Do you have some sunscreen I can borrow?"

Ana shakes her head. But I know she does. She turns to me. "We can stay inside if you want." She looks at the clock. "I have to finish my history homework before class anyway."

"You sure?"

When she walks out of the classroom, I reach into my pocket to make sure my lunch ticket is there.

"I'll just grab my lunch first," I say to Ashley.

She holds up a lunch ticket. "I'll come with you."

We walk into the cafeteria, across the black-and-white checkerboard tile, and join the back of the line. Students slouch, hands in their pockets. The closer we get to the front of the line, the more my face and hands feel the warmth of the heating lamp arched over the food, light bouncing off the foil wrapping. On today's menu: grilled cheese or a hot dog, an apple, and a choice of milk. Mari is showing the new lunch lady, Beatrice, how to scan our tickets.

"No, no, no," Mari says, shaking her head. "The other side. Remember? The barcode."

"Yes, I'm sorry," Beatrice says in an accent I cannot place. She places the red rectangular light of the scanner over the barcode. It beeps. Then her hairnet slides off her forehead, landing on the floor in a droop by her shoes. Mari looks at it and sighs.

Across the cafeteria, I see Ana sitting by herself in a corner, sandwich in one hand, pencil in the other, a textbook open next to her notebook on the table.

It is my turn to order. I slide my tray along the metal bars and hand Beatrice my ticket. I ask for a grilled cheese. Mari, distracted, hands me a hot dog instead, using white plastic tongs to place it on my plate. I lift my tray off the counter, but Ashley stops me, placing her hand in the center of my tray. She does it so forcefully it smacks down on the metal. The milk sloshes in its carton. We all look up.

"Excuse me, but that's not what she asked for," Ashley says now, a little too loud. "You gave her a hot dog." I feel people watching, turning their heads, hear conversations quieting down to a whisper around me. Mari looks at me now, her mouth slightly open, like she wants me to say something.

"Either's fine," I say. "Really."

Ashley turns to me. "No, it's not. That's not what you asked for."

"Sorry," Mari says, picking up the hot dog from my plate with tongs and setting a foil-wrapped grilled cheese on the tray. "Next," she says, avoiding my eye contact. "What would you like?"

"A grilled cheese, please," Ashley says slowly, over-enunciating every syllable. It grates on my ears. My cheeks, I am sure, are red.

"Perdóname," I say to Mari, who nods but does not look at me, like she is giving me the silent treatment with her eyes. I do not know what else to say, or if that was the right thing to say. The right verb. "I'm sorry," I add for good measure.

"I didn't know you speak Spanish," Ashley says while we bring our trays to the table Ana is sitting at. Ana rolls her eyes at me and then turns the page in her notebook. We sit down. "My dad says it is such a useful language to know," Ashley says. "What did you tell her?"

Ashley's dad picks us up after school. The car arrives at the curb in a blur, snow-bright against the dark asphalt. I can see the red leather seats through the lowered windows. A few minutes ago, I borrowed Ana's phone to call mama. I said please, asked her to make up an excuse, an emergency dentist appointment, a sudden, horrible death, but she said it was too late to cancel, just minutes before he was supposed to pick us up.

"Hey, nice to meet you, Sofia," he says as we get into the car.

"Nice to meet you."

He turns to Ashley. "How was school, honey?"

"Good," Ashley says, strapping her seat belt. "Can we stop at the bakery?"

When we get there, her dad drops us off at the curb. Inside, standing in front of the display, the lights overhead illuminate the cupcakes—cookies and cream, strawberry, key lime. A small fly darts from cupcake to cupcake, leaving little indents in the frosting. In the second row: coffee cake with cinnamon swirls, chocolate muffins, lemon squares. It is tempting. I reach into my pocket to make sure my gift card is still there. It is. I look closer.

The strawberry cupcake has silver sprinkles on top that seem to glow in the display case, reflecting the lights above. I decide that I want it but not now. Later, with mama and Rafa.

"I don't think I want anything," I say.

"Oh, okay," Ashley says, bending forward to read a label. "Well, I want something."

She goes up to order. Ashley orders a key lime cupcake for herself and a slice of coffee cake for her dad and a sugar-free biscuit for her grandma. Then she turns and looks at me. "I think he needs to scan it."

"Scan what?"

"Your gift card."

My heart drops. "Oh." I pull it out of my pocket and hand it to the cashier, and it is like I am watching someone else do it instead of me, like it is not my hand holding it out, toward the cash register, not my hand waiting for him to take it. I look at the key lime cupcake, the candied slice of lime wedged into the frosting. He flips over the gift card and scans it. The register spits out a receipt. He hands it to me.

"You have fifty cents left on the card." He backs up from the register and looks at the display case. "If you have another dollar, you might have enough left over for a scone. We have raisin and plain."

I imagine the scone crushed into crumbs in the bottom of my backpack, raisins rolling around in the paper bag. "No thanks. I'll save it," I say, and try to stabilize my voice. I do not want to cry, not here.

When we get in the car, I breathe out slowly, then in, looking out the window. I do not want to cry here either. The farther we drive, the more floors the houses have, two then three then four, and turning left now, we pass by a house with three marble fountains spurting water the color of glass. The water shines for a moment in the sun, pure crystal, before falling back down in a splash. A few minutes later we pull up to a house with a long curved driveway, hedges like big green pom-poms outlining the lawn.

"What do you think?" Ashley says, unstrapping her seat belt.

"It's nice."

She smiles. "I know."

Inside, her dad says he has set up a space for us to study. We walk into the living room, where an L-shaped couch takes up an entire corner of the room. Out in front of it: a circular black coffee table with flared legs. He says he blended blackberries with yogurt and a dash of cinnamon, handing us both dark purple smoothies. No sugar. A white bendy straw arches over the rim of the glass. I take a sip. Tart. I take another sip. Bitter.

"Thank you," I say, and set it back on the table.

"You like it, Ashley?" he asks.

"It's great, Dad. Thanks."

Ashley slings her backpack onto the couch, where it sinks into a cushion. I place mine by the foot of the coffee table. The couch is so bright, so unblemished, I almost do not want to sit on it. I feel something fuzzy brush against my leg and look down. A cat is curling its tail around my ankle.

"That's Muffin," Ashley says, picking him up and placing him on her lap. "Biscuit's around here somewhere."

Muffin, tan with a white belly, jumps out of her lap and scurries under the coffee table. He looks up at me with his green eyes, which, in the shade of the table, shine like two glow-in-the-dark emeralds. I reach my hand out to pet him. He licks my hand with his red sandpaper tongue.

For two hours we go over the next unit, using flash cards to quiz each other on definitions—sedimentary rocks vs. igneous rocks vs. metamorphic rocks—and to describe how wind and water carve canyons, what it means for tectonic plates to shift, the difference between the epicenter of an earthquake and its aftershocks. If I get something wrong, Ashley corrects it gently, casually. No big deal. And so I do the same, not laughing or teasing the way Chloe would when we studied together. I look around the house, at the black-and-white geometric paintings, the gold vase on top of the fireplace, bursting with roses. I wonder if the two of them would get along.

When the snacks are gone and we have finished going over the vocabulary words for not only this unit but the next one, Ashley's dad asks if I want to stay for dinner. He says he already called to check if it was okay. "We're having salmon," he says.

"And garlic bread," Ashley says.

"Okay," I say. "That sounds nice."

I help them set the table. Heavy white plates, shallow crystal bowls for salad, forks, knives, cloth napkins. When we finish setting up the table, an older woman with gray hair walks into the kitchen, slowly making her way across the tiles with her walker. She sets her purse down on the granite countertop, complaining about the traffic.

"Oh," she says, startled, when she sees me. "Company."

"Mom, this is Sofia, Ashley's friend from school," Ashley's dad says, grinding pepper over a bright pink salmon fillet.

She turns toward me. "Are you the one who got the highest score on that quiz?"

"Yes."

"How nice," she says, but the way she says it, it sounds all wrong, sour where sweet is supposed to be. She flicks on the faucet and starts to wash her hands. "You know, before you got here, Ashley won each one of those."

"Granny," Ashley says.

"What? It's true," she says, reaching for a towel.

"I've heard." I smile and try to mean it because mama would tell me that I am a guest in her house and so I should act like it. "You must be proud."

"I am proud. Was prouder before, but," her grandmother says, shrugging. "Well, you know."

Ashley sinks into herself, like the backpack on the couch.

"Mom, come on. Be nice," Ashley's dad says.

"Actually," I say, "I just remembered my mom needed me to call her. Can I call her?"

"Sure. Landline's in the hallway."

When mama picks up, I tell her I want to leave. She sighs and says she will be here in twenty minutes.

When I walk back into the kitchen, I hear Ashley's grandma say, "What? It's not like we aren't paying for at least some of her tuition with our donations. Give me a break."

That night—after mama knocked on Ashley's door and said, "I'm so sorry, I forgot all about Sofia's cello lesson," and Ashley's dad said, "I didn't know you played the cello! What's your favorite chord?" and I said, "All of them," then, unconvincing to even myself, added, "It's hard to choose just one"—mama receives a call from an unknown number. Her phone is charging, the cable plugged into the adapter, when it starts ringing, buzzing in the cup holder.

She picks up. "Hello?"

"Nina, please don't hang up," I hear a voice say. I recognize it. I think again of milk—milk-white. Roundness. Her fingers around my wrist like a cold metal bracelet. Mama presses a button on the phone and sets it face down on the center divider.

"All day, this girl. Look," she says, pulling up the call log. A new call every thirty minutes or so since noon.

"What if it's an emergency?" I think of everything that could have gone wrong. An early birth, all alone. Slipping on the glassy tiles by the shower. Baba.

Mama shakes her head. "That's on her."

When she calls back a few minutes later, mama and I look at each other. She groans. "I'll be back," she says, unlatching her seat belt. She steps outside to take the call.

"What?" I hear her bark into the phone once she shuts the door.

Mama stays quiet for a few seconds, listening. She paces around the parking lot, kicking a rock back and forth between her two feet. Our headlights are two poles of white in the dark, with dust and moths fluttering in the glow. The leaves rustle, whispering to each other—gossiping, maybe, about us. The half-moon, reclining on its side, watches us.

"Nope," mama says. "You knew what—"

She listens again, this time balancing on one of the parking blocks. "No, I'm hanging up now."

"What did she want?" I ask when she gets back into the car.

"For me to come get her," she scoffs. "Give me a break."

"Was it something baba did?"

"What else would it be?" mama says.

"Well, the baby," I say carefully. "Because you're a nurse."

She scowls. "Sleep. Now."

Mama does not want me to know this.

I think she waited until we were sleeping. And I was, for the most part. Rafa, snoring to my left, did not stir once.

What I remember is us pulling up to the driveway of the old house, the click of the car door opening, the thud of it closing, small quiet rustling, the zippery sound of someone strapping on a seat belt. The smell of perfume—earthy and sweet, like sugarplums.

"Thank you, Nina," I heard someone whisper when we drove off. Then again when we parked in front of an apartment complex. "I appreciate it."

Then stillness, then blue morning.

We have fake Spanish class every two weeks. This is what Ana calls it. Today the teacher puts on a sombrero and adjusts a striped red poncho over her dress and rolls a whiteboard into the classroom, a lime-green cactus in a terra-cotta pot bobbing up and down in the tray below the board. The teacher, Señorita Lucy, holds up a picture of an orange. We write "naranja" on lined paper. We do the same with grapes, bananas, lemons.

At lunch, Ana says we do not speak Spanish in fake Spanish class, not really. She says she under-pronounces the words because one time, when Señorita Lucy asked her to read a list of vocabulary words aloud, three boys turned around and made a face, so now she tames the rolled *r*, softens her vowels. She uses words like "bolígrafo" to refer to pens, "bote" to refer to boats. The more she does it, the more she sounds like everyone else, and the less they turn around. I do the same, feeling my grip loosen, letting the vowels and syllables float in front of me, my *r*'s unrolled, unspooling.

After the lunch bell rings, we walk back to the classroom. "You can't just say nothing," Riley tells Cindy, swinging her black-and-white striped lunch bag. The silverware jostles with each swing.

"But what if I haven't done anything wrong?"

"Not a single sin?" Riley makes a face. "I doubt that."

"What are you talking about?" Ana says.

"Confession," says Riley. "It's after lunch. Ms. Clyde wrote it on the board."

I turn to Ana. "Confession?"

"Yeah, you can just say whatever," she says. "I usually say I'm mean to my sisters."

"And then what happens?"

"You repent," she says, like it is obvious. "He has you say a prayer."

"Who does?"

"The priest."

We go row by row, working our way from the front of the classroom to the back. When it is my turn, I get up out of my seat, push in my chair, and walk into a room between the fifth- and sixth-grade classrooms. The room is small, cramped, the size of a closet, and inside are two blue chairs seated across from each other. The door shuts behind me. Father Charles sits with his hands folded over his lap, looking down at his silver watch.

"Hi, Sofia," he says. "Take a seat."

The chairs are so close together our knees touch when I sit. I scoot mine back a few inches. He tells me to do the sign of the cross.

"Anything to share?"

I shake my head. "I don't think so."

"This is a safe space."

I look around and it feels like anything but that—the windows closed like eyes, a shadow swallowing the room whole. "And no judgment," he says. "Just say whatever's on your mind."

"Nothing's really coming to mind."

He is looking at me like he expects me to say something, crossing his arms, but what, I do not know. I hold my breath. I look at the floor, glossy despite the darkness, and focus on the hint of my reflection in the tiles.

"Okay," he says after a minute.

"Okay." I stand up and leave.

Rafa got suspended.

This is why mama is scowling, pulling him by the wrist while I wait in the car. The vice principal, a woman in a striped navy blazer and puffy white dress shirt, walked over to the car during pickup time with the principal and asked mama if she could come with her. They explained that, unfortunately, Rafa had called his teacher a bitch. He would not be allowed to return to school for a week. It is expected that, tomorrow, he will spend a day writing an apology letter to his teacher, the next day writing "I will not curse" in tight, neat cursive, and the rest of the time praying and doing multiplication tables. He coughs into his elbow and then asks for a tissue. I hand him one from my pocket.

"Don't forget the other thing," the vice principal says to the principal now, standing by the car window with her arms crossed.

"Oh, right." The principal nods. "Now that I've got you here, and this isn't so much about Rafa as it is about Sofia," she says, turning toward me. My breath catches in my throat. Mama raises an eyebrow, looking at me. "Don't worry, you're not in trouble or anything, sweetie. It's just that sometimes, when you and Ana speak Spanish, it can make the other kids feel excluded." She brushes something off her forearm. "They said you're gossiping about them. And while *I* know that's not true—"

"We were talking about fruit," I say.

"It really doesn't matter what you were talking about. What matters is it makes the other kids uncomfortable," the vice principal says.

"But we were going over what we learned in Spanish class today," I say, unzipping my backpack. "Are you saying we shouldn't practice our vocabulary words?" I take out the worksheet that Señorita Lucy gave us and hand it to them through the window. While the vice principal flips through it, I think about what Chloe would do if she were here, what she would say. "I guess I'm just confused. I didn't know we weren't allowed to study during recess." Play dumb, Chloe would say. Play dumb.

"Let's just keep it all in Spanish class," the vice principal says to me. She hands me the worksheet.

"But—"

Mama puts a hand on my shoulder. "All right."

"Why didn't you say anything?" I turn to mama when they leave. "I didn't do anything wrong, and you didn't even, I mean, you just let them." I stop, motioning toward the window.

"One suspended kid is enough," she says, then turns to Rafa. "What am I going to do with you? I don't have enough sick days for a week off." She pauses, looks down at her phone, the screen reflecting the top of the car, grabs it, and walks out without saying anything.

"Hi," I can hear her say as she walks away but barely. Rafa and I roll down the windows and crane our necks to hear. "Could you put me through to father?"

"Father?" Rafa turns to me. "Does she mean abuelo?"

She walks out of earshot toward the teacher parking lot and stops by the wooden gate, which is crawling with vines and speckled with small star-shaped blue flowers.

A few minutes pass. While teachers wearing neon-yellow vests help students into their parents' cars, I get an early start on my math homework, sharpening my pencil first. Rafa, sitting to my left, asks for a piece of paper. I rip one out of my notebook. He folds it into a paper airplane and sends it out the window. It glides farther than I expect, landing between the green trash can and blue recycling bin by the dumpster.

"Aren't you gonna go get it?" I ask.

He shakes his head. "Can I have another one?"

I tear out another paper.

Ten minutes later mama approaches the car. "Thank you," she says, reaching for the door. "Thank you, father." She settles into her seat. "Okay," she says. "It's a day now. Only a day."

As soon as I open the car door after school the next day, I can smell the takeout. Greasy, almost sweet. Rafa is squeezing ketchup out of a packet, dipping a fry into the red squirt. The foil crinkles as mama unwraps her hamburger. She shakes her cup, the ice like gravel, and hands it to me. I take a sip. Raspberry iced tea.

"You got burgers?" I ask.

"And ice cream," Rafa says. "We went to the zoo."

"The zoo?"

"Here you go," mama says, handing me a folded-over brown bag. I open it. Underneath a sack of brown napkins is a small flattened hamburger and four or five salt and pepper packets. I take everything out and arrange it on my lap.

"Are there fries?"

Mama looks at Rafa and then starts to laugh like it is some kind of inside joke. "Mijo, you were supposed to share." She hands me a small white box, oily at the bottom. "Take mine."

Rafa coughs before taking a sip of the iced tea. I look down at the straw, practically seeing the germs, then wipe it with my shirtsleeve.

"You went to the zoo?"

Mama nods, her mouth full. "Took the day off."

"You paid for tickets."

"Duh," Rafa says.

"But that's not fair. If I got suspended, you would never," I start but do not know what to say.

"You wouldn't get suspended."

I clench my fists, digging my fingernails into my palms. I cannot help it. I start to cry. Hot tears run down my face, dripping off my cheeks. I turn to the window. I can say the word too. I can call her what he called her a few days ago, right here, up close, to her face. I can do it.

"You're a—" I start. We make eye contact in the rearview mirror. "You're awful."

"Quit it."

I know what I will do. I dry my face with a napkin, wiping my eyes then blowing my nose.

"Finish your dinner," she says.

I look at her phone on her lap and wait.

Later that night, when I am certain she is asleep, deep in her lawn mower snores, I reach across the car for her phone and unlock it. Her password is baba's birthday. I look up abuelo's contact, write his phone number on my wrist, then slide my sleeve down to cover it.

I borrow Ana's phone during recess the next day, crouched in a stall in the girls' bathroom.

The first time I dial abuelo's number, it goes straight to voicemail.

The second time, he picks up.

"Hello?"

"Abuelo, it's me," I say. "Sofia."

"Hello?"

"It's me, Sofia." I speak directly into the phone, as loud as I can without drawing attention to myself. I press the phone closer to my ear.

I hear a chorus of laughter in the background.

"No, it's not a joke," I say. "It's me."

He hangs up.

The third time I call, it rings and rings.

At lunch I ask Ana if I can try again.

"I get charged by the minute, just so you know," she says, pulling the phone out of the front pocket of her backpack and handing it to me.

I dial the number. He picks up.

"Abuelo, wait, don't hang up."

Mama hates me. I know she does. She demanded to see it, my wrist, even though I washed most of the ink off in the bathroom. Abuelo's area code is still there, faintly blue, below my left thumb.

"What the fuck were you thinking?"

She asks if I told him where we were.

I shake my head. "No, I only had a second to talk."

Now her phone is ringing. Abuelo's name flashes across the screen. Rafa asks for a tissue. I hand it to him, then notice the mound of tissues that has accumulated by his feet, piled like dead white flowers around his shoes. He blows his nose into a tissue and tosses it to the floor.

"You gave him my number? Fuck, Sofia," mama says, staring at her phone. "What did you do?"

"At least I'm actually doing something. At least I'm trying."

The phone stops buzzing, abuelo's name fading from the screen. Then a second later he calls again. She tosses her head back, rubs her forehead, and turns it off.

She does not talk to me for two days.

Rafa's coughing wakes us up. Mama presses the back of her hand to his forehead. "Shit."

He groans at her touch. "Everything hurts."

When the library opens mama brings a cup of coffee with her into the computer lounge on the second floor, even though she is not supposed to. She posts an ad for a wedding ring online and a day later has a buyer, who wires her a deposit.

"Now we can get a hotel?" Rafa asks the next day, coughing into his shirtsleeve, wheezing when he breathes in, like an accordion filling with air. We are walking out of the library, stepping from the smooth sidewalk onto the pebbly asphalt of the parking lot, beneath yellow Christmas lights that two men on a red ladder hung up this morning. The librarian said that the lights go up on the same day every year, December fifteenth, ten days before Christmas. Mama printed a confirmation receipt of the wire transfer. It is folded inside my library book. I tuck the book under my arm.

She says the deposit alone is still not enough money to get a hotel room and that any money we get we need to save for a security deposit on an apartment. She looks at Rafa, blowing his nose into a tissue, and lets out a long, slow sigh. She takes her phone out of her pocket.

“I can’t believe I’m doing this,” she says.

She finds abuelo’s contact, presses a button, and holds the phone to her right ear. After a few seconds, in Spanish, mama says we need a place to stay for a few weeks, and yes, it is because of baba, and yes, you were right, and yes, you are always right. Yes, I am sorry. Very sorry. I strain to hear what abuelo says but Rafa is breathing too loudly, blowing his nose into a tissue and then wiping it clean.

A Y-shaped vein pulses on mama’s forehead. She is shaking her head like she cannot believe what she is doing, but I cannot help what I am seeing—the champurrado in the steel olla, abuelo lifting me by the armpits onto the step stool when I was little so I could stir it, handing me the long-necked ladle. The TV in the living room flashing the soccer game, zooming into the ball on the grass, zooming out to the crowd. Abuelo talking sternly to the adults, in his Adult Voice, but stooping down and talking sweetly to me and Rafa, like a bird chirping.

“Sí,” she says every few minutes on the phone, and now, with Rafa asleep, I can hear abuelo’s loud, sharp voice on the other end even though he is not on speakerphone. Mama becomes smaller around abuelo, as if she has shrunk by three feet and is wearing invisible pigtails and has to do what abuelo says when he says it. “Two weeks,” she says in Spanish, her voice quiet. “That’s all I’m asking for. Rafa’s sick.”

She says “Sí” again and then “Yo sé” and “Okay, bye,” and then she turns around to me, startled, and says, “What do you think you’re listening to?” Her pigtails are gone, her height restored.

“Sorry,” I say.

On Saturday morning, mama gives the ring to a bearded man in a leather jacket, who gives her a wad of cash binder-clipped together. After she counts it, flipping the bills in a green blur, she hands it to me. "Double-check it for me." When I tell her it is the correct amount—one thousand four hundred and seventy-five dollars—they shake hands. He puts the ring in his pocket and rides away on his motorcycle, a puff of smoke behind him, like a gray cloud floated all the way from the sky to be here, right here.

We drive for an hour and a half to abuelo's. When we knock on his front door, he runs up to me and Rafa and starts kissing all over our faces. Our cheeks, our foreheads, our noses. He tells mama that he will help her pack us lunches in the morning before we leave. We have gotten so tall, he tells us—what have we been eating that has made us get this tall? He says he needs to know.

"Granola bars," Rafa says, blowing his nose.

"Granola?"

When we get inside, abuelo hides all the granola bars in the house. Honey almond, peanut butter oat, maple brown sugar—gone. He says he will buy us peaches, Rafa's favorite when he was a baby. Mama asks why, and abuelo says that he does not want us to be reminded of the car and the only way to do that is to get rid of all the granola bars.

"Forget about the two weeks," he says to mama in Spanish, squeezing me and Rafa tighter. His white hair, fluffy and clean. Up close I smell his cologne, something bright and outdoors, like pine needles and salt water. A cabin by a blue lake. "Stay as long as you need."

Mama's face darkens for a second. "No," she says. "Just two weeks."

Abuelo's kitchen looks as I remember it only much, much smaller. When I tell mama this later, she says it is because I have gotten taller and that is why I feel like a giant standing here, in front of the sink I could barely reach on tiptoes when I was younger. The bright yellow tiles are still scratched gray from me running from abuela to abuelo, then back again, from chasing Rafa between their towering legs and hiding inside the low-set cabinets, counting to ten in a whisper.

And crouched down here, I remember how the adults heaved hot pans overhead and yelled for the two of us to Stay Put, Goddammit. And For the Love of God, Niños, Take Off Your Shoes. Black pans, the clicking of the stove as it lights, everything seems the same.

I open the sliding doors and walk into the backyard. The breeze tosses my hair back, behind my shoulders. It was Easter the last time we were here. Here, in the garden, I overheard the adults talk about where they would hide the eggs: in between dark gaps in the rosemary bushes, which always looked like stalks of green coral to me, or beneath the grill hood, or in the open mouths of the bubble gum–pink tulips. Abuela filled clear plastic cups with blue, yellow, and red dye, then brought a bowl of hard-boiled eggs and set it on a folding table outside. Baba showed us how to make multicolored eggs, how to use white crayons to etch designs onto the eggshells. I remember the sharp smell of vinegar and how surprised I was that something the color of candy could smell so sour.

After we unload the car, I separate our clothes into piles for mama to wash, whites and darks and colors in mounds by the foot of the bed. We pile onto the bed in the guest room. The quilt, cream white, spread out like a fresh canvas over the mattress. Before we got here, abuelo put a pair of chanclas for each of us by the bed, draped a rosary with beads like pomegranate seeds over one of the pillows. Mama cups the rosary in her hands and pours it into a bedside drawer. Out of sight.

"So, when are we leaving?" Rafa asks a few minutes later, after the three of us sat in the silence of the place, after it became loud—the absence of honking, no tires crunching gravel, no birds chirping, not a single one.

I sit up and face her. I want to stay here. I want to ask mama why we cannot, why this has to be temporary.

Mama sits up and stretches her arms toward the ceiling. "Two weeks. We'll be here for Christmas, mijo. Won't that be fun?" she says, patting his cheek before lifting herself off the bed. "I'm going to see if your abuelo needs any help."

"Why can't we just stay here?" I ask. "I mean, he has space for us," I say, looking around the room.

"Trust me. Okay?"

Just then abuelo knocks.

"I'm on my way," mama calls out. A flash of braids as she closes the door.

Rafa turns to me. "Two weeks is a long time, right?" He is

sitting up now, looking at his backpack. Aside from his clothes, Rafa has not unpacked anything else.

An hour ago, when mama took his school books out from his backpack to help him get settled, he screamed and told her to put them back inside—to close it, close it now, please—and mama stepped back and dropped it. Mama said, "What the hell?" and "Why?" and "What's wrong with you?" He zipped it back up. He said he did not want to empty out his bag just to have to pack his stuff all over again, like he did at Mr. Leonard's. Mama pinched his shoulder. "Don't yell like that again," she said, yelling. I realized I was covering my ears then, when mama looked at me oddly. I lowered my hands.

Now Rafa is looking up at me, waiting for me to answer. "Right?" he asks.

"Yes, I think so."

I unpack the rest of my bag, setting my pencils and eraser on the desk, my library book there too. When I come back to the room after using the bathroom, I sigh, relieved to see Rafa's backpack sitting unzipped in the corner, emptied out. I join them in the living room.

An hour or so later, after the clank and clamor of dishes, the knocking of the knife on the wooden chopping board, the steady whir of the stove fan, abuelo walks toward the couch and says dinner will be ready in half an hour, the albóndigas are still pink in the middle. He puts a hand on my shoulder.

"Ven," he says, and I lift myself off the couch and follow him into his bedroom. The walls in his room are lemon-yellow and the brass lamps—four of them, one in each corner—glow like torches. A painting of the Virgin Mary on the wall across his bed. The gold suns carved into the frame match the ones on her veil.

Abuelo slides the closet door open.

"Mija, agarre los platos?"

"Which ones?"

"Allí. Mira," he says, pointing to the top shelf.

I pull down a stack of yellow plates. Abuelo thanks me, takes the plates with both hands. He starts to walk out of the room but then stops abruptly, and I, right behind him, almost run right into him. Abuelo turns around. "Sofia," he says, holding the dishes to his chest. "¿Por qué siempre me respondes en inglés cuando yo te hablo en español?"

"Oh," I say, feeling my cheeks redden. "No sé." I look down.

The lamp by the door lays its skinny dark shadow across my socks.

Looking at abuelo's face, at the way his lips are pressed into a firm red line, I can tell he wants me to say more. To say it in Spanish. But I do not know what to say, how to tell him that the thought of his disappointment at a less-than-sharp *r*, or God forbid an unrolled one, makes me want to say nothing at all. I open my mouth to speak, but before I can say anything, abuelo shakes his head, disappointed, and walks out the door. The plates rattle with each step.

Abuelo thinks that if he speaks Spanish fast, I cannot understand him, but that is not true. While he and mama wash dishes after dinner I sit at the dining table and pretend I am not listening to their conversation, examining my fingernails, pushing the half-moons of my cuticles back one by one. Abuelo asks mama about baba, about what finally did it, why she left, and mama stays quiet, so quiet, like she herself has become a whisper. Mama leans over the sink to pick up a dirty bowl.

Abuelo asks if she heard his question.

Mama nods and scrubs the bowl until it has become a cloud between her hands, covered in suds.

"¿Pues?"

Mama sighs. "Later, papi."

But abuelo insists, motioning to me and Rafa, saying we cannot understand what they are talking about anyway, and what happened to my Spanish after all? And why did she let me lose it? I want to tell him I can understand him just fine.

Mama runs the bowl under a pale stream of water, the suds sliding off and landing by the drain. Abuelo shuts the faucet off just as Rafa has taken a seat in front of me and spread a deck of Uno cards on the table. A red fan of them.

"Niños," abuelo says, drying his hands with a blue towel.

Rafa and I look up.

He points to the guest room. I help Rafa gather the cards and stuff them into the box. In the bedroom, we sit on the edge of the rug by the door. I tell him to set up the game again and press my ear to the door while he shuffles.

Through the door: in zip-fast Spanish, abuelo telling mama to respond when she is spoken to. That he is her father. It is the least she can do. "Respóndeme, hija," he says, pleading. Then the sound of crashing, something breaking. A glass, or maybe a plate.

Rafa and I barely register the sound of footsteps approaching the door before it swings open. We jump back. Mama runs in. Locks the door. Abuelo pounds on it, saying this is *his* house, *his*. Mama drops her hand from the doorknob and backs away.

"Bed," she whispers.

She turns off the light. Peels back the quilt, the stark white top sheet, and slides into bed. We climb in with her. The way mama is shaking, I think she must be cold, but her teeth are not chattering and her skin feels normal. I brush against her arm while reaching for the blanket.

Eventually, either abuelo stops yelling or I stop hearing it, and either mama stops shaking or she does not, and I fall asleep.

Hunched over a green leather photo album in bed the next morning, wiping her eyes on the sleeve of her shirt, mama says things used to be good.

"Where'd you get that?" I ask.

She ignores me. "See, look," she says, pointing to a picture taped into the corner. In it, baba gives me a bath in a metal kitchen sink when I was a baby, the bubbly water spilling over the edge of the sink like a wave crashing, caught midair in the photo. My mouth is open in a gummy red toothless smile. Mama points to my hair. She says baba used to put shampoo in my hair and sculpt it up, up, like a shark fin. He would make the sound from *Jaws*, "duh-duh, duh-duh, duh-duh-duh-duh-duh-duh-duh-duh-duh-duh," and then he would pretend to hunt me, to catch me in the net of his arms, and I would try and squirm free, squealing, soapy, happy to be caught.

"Things were good," mama says, sniffling. "Do you remember? You loved being a shark."

I do not remember. But she is smiling, so I nod. "The soap would get in my eyes."

She flips to another page. "And in this one—" she starts, then looks up, the jagged metal sound of a key jiggling in the door stopping her short.

Abuelo opens the door, holding up a key chain full of sharp copper and silver keys, like little knives. "Good morning," he says, and stuffs the key chain in his pocket.

Mama tries to shove the photo album underneath her pillow, but abuelo sees it. He walks over and tries to yank it out of her hands. Mama pulls it back, but abuelo pulls harder, and there it is, the crisp sound of paper tearing, a page full of photos landing a few feet away, on the chanclas.

Rafa, startled by the movement, wakes up. Sits up. He looks scared, like he might cry, his eyes wide, glittery, reflecting the light from the open window.

"Oh, no, baby," mama says, reaching for Rafa. "It's okay."

"Déjalo," abuelo says, slapping mama's hands away from Rafa before offering his own.

Rafa backs away from the two of them until there is no more space to do so, until his shoulders are pressed into the headboard. The air turns still. The room holds its breath. The ceiling fan above us stops spinning to watch. I take his elbow and pull him out of the room, through the hallway, and into the living room. I turn on the TV, flipping through the channels until I find a cartoon. I touch his forehead. Feels normal.

"How's your cough?"

"Better."

When abuelo starts up again, I turn up the volume. On the screen, a gray cat chases a mouse through an air vent.

"You want this show or a different one?" I ask.

"This one."

Look what you did, he tells her. You scared Rafa. On a Sunday,

God's day, of all days. Stop thinking about him, he says in Spanish. Stop looking at these pictures. Look at who is in front of you now: your family, your kids. Look at me.

I go to the kitchen to get a glass of water for Rafa, looking out the window while it fills. The flowers by the windowsill, I notice, are wilting. A tulip bulb, there, on the counter, beheaded. Green slime oozes from the stem and drips down the vase.

Tell me something, abuelo says. I grab the remote and turn up the volume so loud, the TV rumbles on the stand.

If he came here and said he was sorry, you'd take him back, wouldn't you? You would, wouldn't you?

Wouldn't you?

Abuela loved baba when she met him. This, abuelo says later that night, should have been the first sign. He says that abuela was a good woman—a good, good woman—but the worst judge of character. He sits next to us on the couch. Mama stares ahead, her face as blank as the wall in front of her. And it is so loud in my ears, what mama would have said otherwise: "She married you, didn't she?" She would have cocked her head the way she does. Eyes bright, mischievous, half joking.

I run my hand along the raised, bumpy pattern of the couch—yellow and red flowers stitched into the brown fabric, papery green leaves lifting off the armrests. Part of me wants to say it for her, to show her I am paying attention, even if it means upsetting abuelo. But what I really want is for mama to do something. Anything. Sigh. Yell. Storm out. When she gets like this, Rafa calls her Statue Mama, the first time being the day baba brought the girl home, when she looked at the girl's belly bulging out of her shirt and became so absolutely still, so quiet, I could not tell if she was breathing. Right now, Statue Mama sits with squared, stiff shoulders, her palms on her knees. A bird could land on her nose and she would not even notice.

Abuelo takes a sip from his mug, coffee with hazelnut creamer, frothy like sea-foam. The way abuelo tells stories, it is like he keeps a long, ancient scroll in his back pocket with him wherever he goes, and, unrolling it now, begins to read. The same stories every time. I can sketch them out, can paint their smallest details with a fine-tip brush, they are that vivid—the dark spots on the yellow corn tortillas, the pink sheen of mama's lip gloss, the calluses on abuelo's hands as he reaches out to shake baba's. It is like I was there. Abuelo sets his mug by the foot of the couch and continues.

The day mama introduced baba to the family, abuela spent all morning making mole, the thick brown sauce simmering into bubbles in the stockpot, the chicken in shreds, falling off the bone. When the doorbell rang, abuela took a deep breath before letting mama and baba inside. Parents get nervous about these things, too, you know, abuelo says, touching his wristwatch.

Abuela hugged mama, then baba, taking the flowers he had brought into her hands: a bouquet of pink and orange carnations wrapped in newspaper, tied with an emerald ribbon, the same color as the stems. Abuelo says he liked the way baba smelled. Fresh. Lemon peel and mint. He shook baba's hand, firm. Abuela motioned for them to come inside.

Mama translated over dinner, turning her head from the left side of the dining table to the right side, then back again, all night. Abuela wanted to know about baba's family. He told her about his mom and four younger brothers who were back home in Cairo, the youngest eleven years old. His oldest brother, Sameh, two years younger than him, was expecting a daughter in a few months and wanted her to be born here, wanted English to be her first language. He said they had already picked out a name for her. "A nice, easy American name."

"Good," abuela said, breaking a tortilla in half.

A few Coronas in, they were all laughing, a little drunk. Abuela pointed to things around the house and asked baba how to say them in Arabic: pointing to the cut-in-half watermelon on the kitchen counter and baba saying, "Batteekh," then pointing to her chair and baba saying, "Korsi." When abuela told him the Spanish words, baba nodded, pronouncing "sandía" and "silla" back to her slowly, then taking a sip from his drink.

"Míralo," abuela said, patting him on the back.

"Very good," said abuelo.

When abuela pointed to her pants and baba said "bantalun," abuela nearly jumped out of her seat and started clapping. "Pantalones! Pantalones!" she said, tugging at her belt loops. The words were practically the same.

Abuelo pulled her back into her seat, smiling, embarrassed. When she was not looking, he took her Corona and hid it under his chair. The rest of the night was like this—words thrown around like Ping-Pong balls, bouncing off the walls in one language, then landing in another, landing everywhere in the house, among the spoons, the shoes, the salt.

Later that night, after coffee and pink conchas, abuela said she was sorry to end their night early, but they had to wake up at six in the morning to go to church tomorrow. "The car's not working, so we'll have to walk," she told mama in Spanish, gathering the dishes. Baba stood up to help, lifting the mugs by their handles in a clink and setting them on the counter.

Abuela turned to abuelo, rubbing his shoulder. "Vamos a despertar tempranito mañana."

"Sí," abuelo said, then turned to baba. "Car is broken."

"You know, I can take a look at it if you want," he said to

mama, collecting the spoons even though abuela shooed him away, motioning toward his chair for him to sit down.

"Korsi," abuela said.

"He knows cars, mami," mama said, grabbing baba's hand on the dining table and interlacing their fingers. "He's good at these things. It's his job."

"She's right," said baba.

A few minutes later, abuelo and baba were elbow-deep under the hood of his blue pickup truck, grease streaking their forearms and cheeks and noses like smears of black paint, motor oil in dark puddles on the concrete floor of the garage. Abuelo held the flashlight over baba while he dug through the toolbox in his trunk, the wrenches and screwdrivers in there scratched with use, orange with rust. He wore one of abuelo's old white undershirts because abuela insisted he not get his nice button-down dirty, and when he declined, saying he had stain remover at home, she pulled the neck of abuelo's undershirt over his head like he was a baby and told him that was nonsense, to put it on. He looked at mama, who shrugged at him, smiling shyly. "Okay. Thank you," he said, putting his arms through the holes. The shirt hung loosely on his body, the fabric in folds under his armpits.

"Good," abuela said, patting his head.

Meanwhile, in the kitchen, mama washed the dishes while abuela dried them.

"Mira," abuela said, towel in hand as she shook her head, pointing to a grain of rice wedged in between two prongs of a fork.

"Sorry."

Mama took the fork and scrubbed it clean with the rough

back of the sponge. The water streamed out of the faucet in a soft hush, dulling the clanks of metal and laughter coming from the garage. Mama asked abuela what she thought about baba. She paused, putting the plate she was drying back on the counter. She said it was too early to tell.

"What do you mean, too early to tell?" mama asked in Spanish, lathering a slotted spoon. "He's been here for hours. He's there, outside with papi, helping him. Helping you."

"Hand me a new towel from the drawer, mija? This one's soaked."

"Mami," she said, shutting off the water. "Don't do that. Don't ignore me."

"What? I already told you. It's too early to tell."

At nine thirty, they called it a night. Baba said he would come back tomorrow to finish, once he picked up a few parts from the auto shop across the street from the gas station. They were not open on Sundays. "But I know the owner," he said. Baba would drive them to church in the morning. When abuela asked if he wanted to join them, he hesitated, looking again at mama, who explained that baba was not Catholic.

"What is he, then?" abuela said, looking at mama suddenly, a hand over her chest.

"Coptic Orthodox," said mama. "Christian, like you, mami. It's the same thing."

"Is it?"

"Close enough," said mama.

"Come with us to church tomorrow?" abuela asked in English.

"Mami."

"What? It's just a question."

To mama's surprise, baba nodded. "I'll pick you up at eight?"

After hugs and kisses goodbye, a sturdy handshake from abuelo to baba, they drove back to baba's apartment, where mama looked through his closet to find another dress shirt for him to wear the next day. When they could not find one, they drove to a department store, got there fifteen minutes before closing, and went straight to the sales rack.

The next morning, he walked up to abuela's house wearing a plaid blue shirt with a solid black tie and tan pants, mama stepping out of the car wearing a long, ruffly yellow dress with a knit shawl covering her shoulders. After church, abuela made breakfast while abuelo helped baba unload the parts from the car. They had eggs and refried beans, which abuela served with both corn and flour tortillas she warmed on the comal.

It was one thirty when they finished the car. Abuela insisted they stay for lunch, then later, at five, for dinner. Mama cooked something baba taught her how to make, beef and green beans stewed in tomato sauce and onions, served over rice. Abuela nodded in approval after her first bite, dotting her face with a napkin. The next day, she called to ask for the recipe.

"Your abuela was convinced," abuelo says in Spanish, looking at me, tapping his fingers on the armrest. "You know what she said? She said, 'Finally, I have a son.'" Abuelo looks sad for a moment, staring into his mug, empty now. "But none of that matters anymore," he says, pushing himself off the couch.

Abuelo stops a few feet from us on his way to the kitchen. He balls his left hand into a fist. Then he grunts and takes the mug in his right hand and slams it onto the floor. Rafa gasps. I cover my face. Abuelo continues into the kitchen, pours himself a glass of water, and walks toward his bedroom like nothing happened. The shards from the yellow mug scattered like petals around our feet. Mama blinks.

He leaves us here alone, me, Rafa, and a statue.

"Oh my god," I say. "Oh my god."

On Monday, we leave at five thirty in the morning to make it to school by eight. "Morning traffic," mama explains to abuelo, who is bent on one knee by the front door, helping Rafa tie his shoes, his foot on a faded spot of abuelo's jeans. Rafa steadies himself by grabbing on to the coat rack. He is holding his breath. I can tell because his cheeks are puffed up, full of air, slightly pink. I have been holding my breath too. All weekend, it feels like. This morning, I found a few yellow specks of mug in my hair. I swing my backpack over my shoulders and pull the black straps down to tighten it, then slip on my shoes. When abuelo asks her what time we will be back home and mama says six, maybe seven, I look over at her, confused for a second, because school ends at three.

"That late?" Rafa asks.

"Traffic."

"Hm," abuelo grunts, making one last loop with Rafa's shoelaces and then pulling it into a bow. "You can take the shortcut," he says, mentioning a street I do not know. "So you can get home faster."

"They closed that street," she says.

"No, they didn't. I used it yesterday."

"There's construction."

"Since when?"

When we get into the car, mama lets out a long, slow breath, a whole belly's worth of air. I can smell the coffee in her breath, the hazelnut in the creamer. It fogs up her window, blurring the red mailbox, the trunk of the maple tree, abuelo's blue pickup truck. The way her shoulders relax, lowering from her ears, I can tell she is glad to be out of the house. Rafa is, too, his breathing back to normal. I lean my head on my seat belt strap. Mama starts the car.

We get to school at seven. For an hour until the morning bell, the three of us sit in silence, watching pink clouds bloom like peonies above the dark mountains. A hare scurries across the grass and three babies follow clumsily behind her, their white cotton ball tails bright as headlights as they cross the street.

After morning prayer, Ms. Clyde announces that our class will play white elephant before school lets out for Christmas break on Friday. Ana waits until she has her back turned to us before passing me a note: "Why does everything have to be white? Even elephants." I look over at her and give her a weak smile, though I do not feel like it. Ms. Clyde taps two fingers on our desks as she passes by.

"Pay attention, girls," she says.

"Pay attention, girls," Ana repeats nasally, her thumb and index finger pinched over her nose. The class laughs. Ms. Clyde whips her head back and gives her detention right then and there.

"It was worth it," Ana tells me in line for recess, holding a pink detention slip.

Ms. Clyde explains the rules of the game after lunch. First, everyone brings a present to class—with a fifteen-dollar limit, she adds, looking at John-Isaac, whose parents had purchased a brand-new limited-edition gaming console, three controllers, and a monitor for his older brother's contribution to white elephant last year. John-Isaac shrugs. "Anyway," Ms. Clyde continues.

She says the day of the game, each of us will draw a number from a hat and take turns choosing presents to open, going in numerical order. She says people can "steal" each other's gifts up until the very last round.

Abuelo buys me a watercolor set from the drugstore so I can participate. I tell him he does not have to, but he swats the thought away as if it were a fly. "You have to show them you're just like them, mija," he says in Spanish, handing it to me, a glittery red bow pressed on top of the copper wrapping paper. He wrapped it himself. I want to tell him that, if I could have anything for Christmas, it would be this.

After school on Friday, I come home with a leather journal, a teal feather pen tucked inside. I had swapped the horseshoe charm bracelet I unboxed in the first round for a friendship bracelet kit with turquoise beads and rainbow-colored thread, then swapped it for the journal and pen. We were not allowed to choose the gifts we brought with us. I show it to mama, who nods, then to abuelo, who says I did good, going in with something that costs a few dollars and leaving with something that costs much more.

Rafa points to the journal. "That used to be a cow, you know." He takes the journal from the kitchen counter and lifts it up to his nose. "Smells like one."

"Hey," I say, taking the journal back.

"What?"

And he grins, his cheeks as plump as the peaches on the counter. I look over at mama. She is staring out the window, beyond the leaf-littered driveway, the dry maple leaves curled up like dead bugs. She is looking at the car. Head resting on the wall, looking at it longingly, the way people in the telenovelas look at each other.

When mama gets up to use the restroom a few minutes later, I walk toward the table by the front door. I stare at her car keys. Then I hear the toilet flush, the water gush out of the sink. Quickly, I take her keys and put them in my pocket. Tomorrow, in the morning, I will put them back there, on the table, when it is time to go to school.

Ever since we got to abuelo's, watching mama smile is like watching a puppet show, like watching someone else pull the strings, tugging her eyebrows, the corners of her lips, the roundness of her cheeks, up, up. She smiles like she is trying to smile. I can tell because her eyes are all wrong—her eyes two artificially lit rooms. Fluorescent bulbs instead of daylight. There is a difference. I see it happen now as I hand her my math quiz, an A on top circled in red.

"That's nice," she says.

I put it back in my folder, wondering, for a second, if her smile would be real, teeth and lips, if I had gotten an A+ even though Ms. Clyde does not give out anything higher than an A.

"I'll be right back," I say, and take my folder with me. "Going to the bathroom." I walk to our bedroom, grab a red pen from the mug full of pencils on the desk, then rummage through my folder for last week's English quiz. When I find it, I use the red pen to add a skinny plus sign near the A, trying my best to mimic the slightness of Ms. Clyde's handwriting. I take it with me to the living room.

"Look," I say, showing her the quiz.

She glances up.

"This one's from English class," I say.

"Nice." Same puppet smile.

"She's a tough grader, you know."

"I know."

I take the paper back. "You don't even care," I say. "If Rafa got an A+, you'd throw a party. You'd—" I fold the quiz, trying not to cry. "You'd get him whatever he wanted."

I crumple the paper, walk back into the bedroom, and slam the door. I sit up in bed with my arms crossed, the quilt a tangled mess by my feet. I wait for mama to knock, to come in, to sit down next to me with a box of tissues. I wait for her to come into the room with a brush and comb through my hair and maybe even braid it, like she did when I was younger. Instead, the sun sets. The sky blushes a fierce scarlet, embarrassed, and I feel it on my cheeks, its warmth.

After dinner, I pull the cord on the lamp in our room and get the photo album out from under the bed. Oily fingerprints dot the green cover. When I open it, the loose page falls out, landing face down on the sheets. I turn it over. There are two photos on the page, the glare of tape on the corner of each photo.

The photo on top: Baba bent over a brown suitcase, holding Rafa to his hip.

I bring the picture closer. The suitcase looks old, tattered. There is a dark stain toward the bottom, by the front zippered pocket. It might be the same suitcase he brought when he moved here. I know he was in his twenties when he left Cairo. When he moved here, it was with more sweets than clothes, he liked to say. Teta had wrapped a floral cloth around a tray of fayesh and stuffed it into his suitcase, telling him to return the cloth when he returned to Egypt. The cloth is at home in the drawer closest to the sink, folded into a triangle. It has a red flower in the middle, clustered by green leaves and yellow buds.

Teta had packed him zalabya in a metal tin, basbousa in foil, and a large plastic bag of chocolate cookies she had cross-hatched with her fork, he said. The holy water, which she arranged to be blessed by the abouna at the church, had spilled all over his clothes, he realized, the suitcase dripping as he rolled it out of the airport. He said he wanted to bend down to fix it, but the airport was so crowded, there was no room.

Amo Sam and his two sons picked him up from the airport. "Say hi," amo Sam said to the two boys, helping baba fit his wet suitcase in the trunk. Baba said he remembers how they pressed their faces to the glass, knowing he brought presents for them. The four of them finished most of the zalabya on the ride to amo's house, sticky fingertips all of them.

"Where's the snow?" baba asked him in Arabic.

Amo laughed. "What snow? It doesn't snow here."

"But the movies."

"Not here, no. Other parts, yes." He shook his head, smiling. "English, habibi."

Baba would stay with them and amo's wife, Nadine, at the apartment on Lemonbalm Street until he got his own place. He said amo was his cousin, but baba said everyone was his cousin—people we would run into at the market, a man waiting at the bus stop with a plastic bag full of pears, the woman who rode her bicycle around our neighborhood on Sundays tossing rolled-up newspapers onto the front steps. All of them cousins.

At the house he handed the boys presents: a pack of plastic-wrapped pyramids, two wooden cars with rubber wheels, and a camel doll with long eyelashes and a red saddle over its humps. He showed us a picture once. "Toys were simpler then," he would tell us. When he called home the next day, teta asked him to mail prenatal vitamins for his cousin, a box of chocolate-covered almonds in plastic wrap for one of the abounas at the church, insoles for giddo, and perfume samples for giddo's sister, whom teta said needed them badly. Baba always pinched his nose when he said this. Rafa laughed.

When amo Sam and tunt Nadine showed him around, baba said they stopped speaking to him in Arabic. His English was not good enough yet, they told him, even though he had won a school-wide English essay contest a few years earlier—the best essay about family written in his school. In English, they showed him step by step how to make basbousa out of Cream of Wheat. They wrote walking directions to the Lebanese market a few streets past the highway, which sold discounted meat on Fridays. Amo Sam introduced him to amo Rodger, a man in his fifties who was a deacon at the church and owned a gas station where baba would work. "For now, at least," amo Sam said. "Until you get settled."

He said amo Rodger wanted sons but only got daughters—got pink where he wanted blue, he would say—and then there was baba on the first day of work, wearing a bright blue polo shirt. He greeted him with a wide smile. Baba kept a list of helpful phrases Nadine had written out by hand for him folded up in his pocket. He liked that amo Rodger spoke to him in Arabic. He said he still remembered the first time he had to help a customer, the deep blush of English.

"Bathroom? Over there," he said, reddened.

Baba painted on the weekends, saving money from his shifts at the gas station to buy sample-size paint cans from the home-improvement store. He knocked on restaurant doors and asked if he could repaint their signs, assuring them first that he would not charge much. He spent his days off outlining the lettering in black, touching up the corners, adding fresh coats of varnish for restaurants all over the city. A few weeks later, when he could afford to, he purchased an expensive set of oil paints, a pack of canvases, a wooden easel, and a set of brushes made from horsehair, but he hardly had time to use them, he was so busy with work. "I don't know," he said when amo Sam asked him what he wanted to do when he moved on from the gas station. "I just want to paint."

When amo Rodger died five years later, slumped over the cash register in a heart attack, baba learned that he had left him the gas station. This was the year before mama pulled up to it. He decided to sell the gas station to someone else at church and used the money to move out and rent a small studio apartment, where baba had one of each thing: one pan, one bowl, one fork. The first thing mama ever bought him was a set of ceramic teacups. He never touched them. Mama says it was rude of him to leave them there, ignored on the shelf, but baba said it was because he wanted them to look like that for as long as possible, unchipped, brand new.

I turn the knob on the lamp, brightening it, and then look down the page.

In the other photo: teta with a streak of flour on her cheek, Rafa sitting next to her on the couch, chewing on a wooden spoon. I remember that day—teta in a black dress, black headscarf, black shoes—bent over a tin bowl in our kitchen a few years ago, rolling yellow dough into a smooth, tight ball. Her fingers were shaking. They always had but now it was her hands, her forearms too.

Mama said she had Parkinson's. Two strokes. Two bad falls. But baba could not talk her out of it—she was intent on preparing food for me and Rafa. I had not seen her since she last visited from Egypt. And now there she was, leaning forward on the counter, making fayesh. My favorite.

In Arabic she told us to eat, pushing a plate of breaded chicken toward us, which she had burnt herself frying. On her wrist was a small red welt, like a stamp of lipstick. There was onion rice warming in a metal pot on the stove, a potholder on top of the handle.

"Eat," she said again, in English this time. It was one of the few words she knew how to say in English.

Rafa and I looked at each other. It would be rude not to, our eyes seemed to say. I handed him a plate, a fork. I said "thank you" in Arabic, one of the few words I knew how to say. "Shukran."

Teta had grown thinner, more frail since I had last seen her. This was not the teta I remembered, who would take us on long, uphill walks, shouting down the dogs that barked at us as we walked past them. "Bas," I remember her repeating until they would settle, backing away from the gate with lowered tails, whining.

This was not the teta who would hand me a plastic grocery bag to hold open while she gathered fruit from strangers' front yards—strawberries overflowing onto the sidewalk, teta stooping down to collect them like jewels that fell out of a purse. She plucked green crabapples from bushes, yanked blood oranges from high-up tree branches that looked like outstretched hands, offering her the fruit. I dropped them into the plastic bag until it stretched like a full stomach. She did not care who saw.

The picture does not capture her hands quivering as she spooned turmeric out of a repurposed jar. Or mama and I reaching over to help.

"La," she said, swatting our hands away. "No."

When the fayesh finished baking, I ate it the way I always did, by dipping it into Lipton tea that was pale with milk and sugar. I watched the fayesh expand in the tea, swelling like a yellow sponge until it became too soaked to lift out of the mug in one piece.

I close the photo album. I take it to abuelo's room and put it high on the shelf, under a pile of abuela's church dresses. When I rearrange the dresses, they cough dust at me.

At school, Ana likes to play a game called Don't You Hate It When. At lunch today, the last day of school before Christmas break, it is "Don't you hate it when kiwi gets like this?" and she pulls the red lips of the ziplock bag open like a mouth. The kiwi looks like thin slices of jade, shiny and pale.

"What's wrong with it?" I ask, using a spoon to scoop out the last of the blueberry yogurt that abuelo packed in my lunch box.

"It's all slimy," she says like it is obvious, wrinkling her nose.

"I bet it still tastes good, though."

She frowns and zips up the bag, then tosses it back into her lunch box. She puts her head down. "I hate when that happens," she says. "Don't you?"

Don't you hate it when it is leftover night? Don't you hate it when you can't choose the movie? Don't you hate it when your mom asks you to rinse the rice three times, like it is some kind of baptism? Don't you hate it when this, when that, when too much or too little? Sometimes I want to walk away, but then who would I sit with at lunch? I look around the cafeteria and see Ashley sitting by herself, reading a book.

Ana sits up, grabs a small pink coin purse shaped like a clam from her lunch box, then slides the bag of kiwi over to me. "All yours," she says.

"You sure?"

I feel bad for a moment, wondering if she could see it on my face, what I was thinking. She walks over to the vending machine, slips in a few quarters, and stoops down to pull out a bag of chocolate chip cookies. I finish the kiwi before she returns.

"Want to sit with them?" she asks, pointing to a group of sixth and seventh graders sitting underneath the monkey bars. Antonio is on top of the slide talking to them, and it reminds me of Father Charles, how he moves his hands while he preaches.

"Sure," I say.

There is something glittery in the air, as if snowflakes are falling around us, shimmering the morning. Christmas is in five days. Earlier today, after the morning prayer, the principal went from classroom to classroom wearing a Santa hat with yellow string lights wrapped around it. She rang a bell and said, "Ho, ho, ho!" while walking into our classroom with a pitcher full of hot chocolate. The vice principal followed right behind her, carrying paper cups and mini marshmallows, wearing a droopy green felt hat, dressed like an elf. The sugar has kicked in, I think, watching the kids play outside, chasing basketballs at full speed across the court.

When we walk up to the monkey bars, Ana nudges me in Antonio's direction. "There he goes again," she says, annoyed, but there is something more in her voice, a hint of a smile.

Antonio likes to tell stories about when he was little, stories from before he was born, and today—maybe it is the hot chocolate—he can hardly sit still. A small crowd has gathered around him, sitting cross-legged underneath the striped shade of the monkey bars.

Even Mr. Yoon and Mrs. Gonzalez, the second- and eighth-grade teachers, are here, standing by the swings, listening.

Yesterday, Antonio said his mom swallowed a cherry lollipop whole, stick and all, when he was in the womb. "That's why my tongue is bright red," he said, sticking it out for us to see.

"Oh," said a first grader.

And the day before that, he told us about how he was a cloud thirteen years ago. He said he made it hail outside the train station so his parents would meet, and it worked—a man offered an umbrella to a woman, she looked up at him, and that night, they made him. "That same night," he said, patting the bench next to him for emphasis.

"And one time, when I was little, these hornets made me a necklace," he says now, taking a sip of hot chocolate, a mini pink marshmallow sticking to his upper lip. I sit on the swing next to Ana, my feet dangling above the sand. "Eight or nine of them landed around my neck. I thought I was going to die. I mean, these hornets were," he says, looking around. "They were as orange as those things over there." He points to the traffic cones lining the teacher parking lot. "But when they left, the hornets were see-through. And there was an orange necklace around my neck. They gave it to me. They gave me their color."

"I don't believe you," a third grader holding a half-eaten ham-and-cheese sandwich says, crossing her arms.

"Yeah," says someone behind me. "Prove it."

"Oh, well, do you want proof?" he says, smiling, and I can tell that this is his favorite part. The reveal. Ana leans in, eyes wide.

He lifts the collar of his shirt, revealing an orange cord necklace. From here, it looks like a long neon shoelace. The younger kids gasp. Ana smiles. Then he lifts the necklace over his head, walks over to me, and drapes it around my neck. He rests his hand on my collarbone. My right ear warms where his hand glides past it. I notice I am holding my breath even though I do not mean to. He is right in front of me, looking at me, the sunlight melting the dark brown of his eyes, softening it. I blink. I touch the necklace, then turn to face Ana. To my right, an empty swing seat rocks forward, then back. Forward, then back.

On Christmas Eve, while mama reads a newspaper on the couch, her feet on the armrests, and while Rafa uses a trowel to dig around the roots of the lime tree in the backyard, looking for bugs, abuelo calls me into the dining room. Outside, in the garden, tomatoes hang like heavy red ornaments from the vines.

Abuelo is standing behind a large plastic container full of pinto beans on the dining table, patting the blue lid. I hold the bottom of the container with both hands as he tips it out over the table. The beans pile on top of each other, a mound of small spotted pebbles. Abuelo takes a seat then motions for me to do the same across from him.

We sort through the beans, picking out the hollow skins, the small sharp rocks.

Abuelo says that at dinner one time, when he was young, his older sister bit down on a rock that made it into the olla despite the sorting and chipped her two front teeth. He says all the boys in the neighborhood called her "linda" after that—"pretty"—even though her name was Ines. They rode their bikes right up to her on the sidewalk, ringing their bells. "Linda, Linda, Linda," they taunted, until she cried and ran home, covering her mouth the whole way. Soon enough, everyone in the family called her Linda, including him. When I tell this to mama later, asking if it is true, she nods. "Oh, yes, tía Linda," she says quietly. "Kids can be so mean."

We are almost done sorting the beans when abuelo finds a dead beige moth in the pile. He scoops it into his hands and brings it outside to Rafa, who digs a hole with the trowel and buries it beneath the lime tree.

We put the beans in a large stockpot to soak overnight. He says they are for tomorrow. "For Christmas."

On Christmas morning, Rafa drags his feet as he walks toward mama, the shuffle of his slippers, soft whispers against the hardwood floor.

"Can I ask you something?" he asks, sitting down next to her on the couch.

"Of course."

"And you won't get mad?"

She shakes her head. "I won't."

"You promise?"

"Promise."

Rafa pauses. "Did you get presents for us?"

"Oh," she says, glancing over at the Christmas tree, which abuelo spent all morning stringing up with pointy lights that twinkle red-blue-green before leaving for church with his neighbor a few minutes ago. Abuelo had stopped celebrating holidays when abuela died, kept his house dark and undecorated on Halloween, his grill shut on Fourth of July, saying it did not feel right without her there, but mama convinced him to give us Christmas this year, helping him haul the plastic tree section by section out of the garage and into the living room.

"I did, but," mama says, then sighs. "It's small." Then she rises up from the couch, walks over to the tree, and bends down to pick up a small box wrapped in silver-and-gold-striped paper. She hands it to us. "It's for both of you," she says. Rafa starts to rip off the paper as soon as it leaves her fingers. "Wait, never mind, don't."

"Soap," Rafa says, holding it up, the wrapping paper torn off into gleaming scraps by his feet. He slouches, disappointed.

"It's a nice one," she says. "It's for both of you."

He does not even pretend to like it or smile or at least say "Thank you," and I wish he would because now mama is looking away from us, toward the wall on the opposite side of the room, rubbing her neck. She starts to sniffle, holding it in. I can tell because she tries to breathe in deeply, but her breath does not seem to make it that far, catching in her throat.

"Next year, I'll," she starts, wiping her eyes. "Next year will be better."

I take the bar from him.

"Royal Melon," I say, reading the label. I bring the bar up to my nose. "Rafa, smell," I tell him. "It smells good."

"No thank you."

I take him by the hand and walk to abuelo's bathroom.

"What are you doing?"

"Just use the soap."

I turn on the faucet and watch as Rafa rubs the bar between his hands until a foamy lather starts to form. I do the same. Then we rinse it off under the cold stream of water, smelling our hands after, which smell all royal, all melon.

"Tell her thank you and go give her a hug," I tell him, handing him a towel.

After he dries his hands, I follow behind as he walks over to her. "Go on."

"Thank you," he says, looking down at his feet.

She sniffles. "You really like it?" Her eyes are wet, shiny like sea glass.

I nudge him.

"Smell my hands," he says. He offers them to her.

"Food's getting cold," mama calls out from the dining room later that night.

"Coming," I say.

Walking toward the dinner table, I feel my mouth start to water. Chile verde topped with sprigs of fresh cilantro. Enchiladas sprinkled with grated cheese. An olla full of refried pinto beans—no rocks, we double-checked. All with the hand-carved wooden serving spoons that mama got abuela for her birthday a few years ago, the handles arched over the side. Four plates, ready. Knives, forks, napkins. Even a skinny vase of petunias in the center. The white petals flare out like fireworks.

"Is this all for us?" Rafa asks.

Abuelo nods toward the food as if to say, Of course.

We serve ourselves, the wooden spoons going from me to mama to Rafa to abuelo and all the way around again. Rafa eats ravenously, stuffing forkfuls of food into his mouth. Abuelo glances up from his plate. "Mijo," he says to Rafa, laughing. He tells him to eat slow, like me, and I look down at my fork, unaware that I was eating slowly.

"Déjalo," mama tells abuelo, reaching across the table for a napkin, then handing it to Rafa. "I mean, come on, it's Christmas. Let him eat how he wants."

Rafa and I look at each other, then at abuelo, who clears his throat, then nods. Rafa serves himself another ladle full of chile verde, humming to himself. I breathe out through my nose.

Normally on Christmas, we spend the afternoon with the Egyptian side of the family and the evening with the Mexican cousins from the South who fly in for the holidays. I wonder what baba is telling amo about where we are, why we could not make it to his party this year. Maybe baba took the girl to amo's house instead. If she found her way back to him. I can picture it: baba wearing the same striped gray button-down shirt he wears on Thanksgiving, Christmas, and Easter and the girl squeezed into one of mama's nice red dresses, stretching out the fabric. My mouth sours at the thought, at how easily replaceable we might be—same clothes, different people—and I put my fork down. It clanks on the plate, louder than I would like. Everyone looks up.

"What's wrong?" mama asks.

I pick my fork back up. "Nothing."

Last Christmas, we walked into amo's house with arms full of presents: remote-controlled fire trucks with long detachable water hoses, blond dolls stuffed into sequined gift bags, digital cameras. Rafa picked out the wrapping paper. White snowflakes against a wintry blue sky.

Mama bought video games for the older cousins, scratching off the warning labels before wrapping them so they would not get in trouble with their parents for playing. "What's so bad about *The Sims*? It's not gory or anything, right?" she asked the cashier at the video game section of the department store after learning that my fourteen-year-old cousin, Andrew, was not allowed to play video games rated thirteen and older. The cashier shrugged, scanning the barcode.

The adults sat on the couch sipping Lipton tea, dipping fayesh into their glass mugs with their backs to a framed portrait of Abouna Shenouda. Mama and baba pulled up chairs to join them while Rafa and I went into the kitchen and piled plates with kofta, charred on the grill and still warm, and scoops of rice and fresh toasted pita. We got a smaller plate for the basbousa, lifting a square off the platter with a spatula, an almond pressed into the center of each slice.

When we finished eating, we looked for our cousins, who were in the backyard, arguing about who would get to be Mary when we acted out the nativity scene—who was pure enough, unkissed, unlooked at by boys. "I only have one boy in my class, and he doesn't even notice the rest of us. All he cares about is Legos," my cousin Mariam said. The rest of the girls and I looked at each other. We could not compete with that. I had eleven boys in my class. The rest of us, it was decided, would be shepherds. The youngest kids, sheep. The wise men, the three boy cousins with the highest grades. Joseph, the oldest boy.

When Mariam became Mary, she went to the nursery room and lifted her little brother, only a few months old, from his crib, cradling his head to her chest with a light blue blanket. She stood next to Joseph and stuffed a pillow into her shirt, rounding her stomach. The sheep baa'd, cupping their hands around their mouths. The wise men were wise, muttering things about statistics and probability. Joseph knocked on a few bedroom doors, making his rounds around the house, and after Mary complained of contractions, she went into labor, and Jesus was born, spittle hanging from his mouth and dripping down the length of his safari animal onesie. Mary, exhausted from the labor, became Mariam again and laid her brother back in his crib before suggesting we play cards.

After a few hours, we said goodbye and drove home, past inflated snowmen with drooping carrot noses, past reindeer statues twinkling on front lawns. Mama's cousins landed at the airport just before we left amo's house. "They're almost here," she said, turning into our driveway.

They rang the doorbell half an hour later. After hugs, after kisses, with José Feliciano playing at full volume, rumbling the entire house with his radio-crackled belting, all of us crowded around the kitchen island, our hands washed, aprons on. We made red, green, and dessert tamales, folding the hojas over the masa, each one like its own present to unwrap.

While they steamed, we opened real presents, the adults walking around the house with trash bags, stuffing them with wrapping paper the second it touched the floor. Mama walked into the living room balancing a tray of mugs filled with hot chocolate, handing one to each of us. Everyone spent the night at our house but left the next morning to stay with abuelo for the rest of their trip, until New Year's, because he insisted on seeing them while they were in town.

"Tía Linda and her kids couldn't make it this year?" I ask mama now, who is piling small bones from the chile verde from her plate into a white porcelain bowl.

"Not this year, no," she says.

"They will next year," abuelo says. "Next year, we'll have Christmas all together, all day, like we're supposed to."

After dinner, abuelo hands us each a card with two twenty-dollar bills inside and a handful of scratchers for good luck, a penny for each of us. Mama says she will hold on to the cash for us. Reluctantly, I hand her my card and watch her slip the cash into her wallet.

"It's mine, though, right? The money?"

"Of course," she says, zipping her wallet closed.

Rafa and I sit cross-legged on the floor, using the pennies on the scratchers, the copper glinting in the Christmas tree lights. We do not win. Rafa is disappointed.

"It's okay. No one wins anyway," I say, rubbing his shoulder.

Abuelo doesn't want us to leave, but mama says we have to. Mama has good news for us. An after-Christmas gift of good news, not wrapped or tied with a bow but still good. She got a year-end bonus at work. With this extra bit of money, plus what she got from selling the ring, she says we can afford to live in the low-income housing section within, but not necessarily considered a part of, the homeless shelter close to school. This is the real present: a place. She shows us pictures of the unit online—walls the color of honey, a dining table made of dark wood, four matching chairs, and in each of the two bedrooms, a metal bunk bed, a closet, and a bedside table with a drawer. A furnished apartment. A sink. A shower. A gas-lit stove.

We leave in three days, she tells us.

The evening before we leave, abuelo tosses my jacket to me and says he and I are going on a walk. I am sitting at the dining table, where I have spread out the math packet Ms. Clyde assigned us over break. I look down at my pencil. I want to tell him I have to finish this assignment, but he is standing right here, by the table, telling me to put on my jacket. I glance around us. No mugs in sight. No plates. Nothing but my pencil. I place my hand over it.

"I can't."

He takes the jacket from my hands. He unzips it forcefully, holding it open for me to slip my arms through.

"No, I can do it," I say.

We walk outside. The traffic light blinks green, and he insists on holding my hand while we cross the street, letting go when we reach the sidewalk. It is only four thirty p.m., but I am walking through ink, the sky is so dark. I ask where we are going.

After a few minutes, we reach the main street, lit with boxy lamps. We walk past the church with the Virgin Mary statue to the left of the entrance, her palms pressed together, eyes closed, thin black eyelashes painted down to her cheeks. There are vases of roses at her feet, some so freshly cut I can smell their perfume.

Abuelo does the sign of the cross as we pass by. We turn the corner and walk two more blocks. Past the elementary school, past the liquor store with a flashing neon-yellow sign shaped like a lightning bolt. Abuelo turns toward the panadería.

Inside, he grabs a plastic tray and a set of metal tongs, setting three conchas on the tray—a pink one, a brown one, and a white one. He says I loved these when I was little. Then he tells me to get a pack of corn tortillas, and I am surprised at how warm the bag is when I grab it, steam puffing up the plastic like a balloon. Abuelo tells me they make them here, fresh in the back. He tells me to get a pack of flour tortillas, too, and by the time I have returned he has arranged a whole tray of pan dulce. Bright yellow cookies with red icing smiles, custard-filled pastries, flaky orejas.

He pays in cash, snapping his wallet open, then counting the bills slowly. We squeeze our way out the door, past a line that has formed around the block, people in coats waiting for menudo, bringing their own pots, their own lids.

We take the long way home.

Abuelo points out the secondhand furniture store and says this is where he and abuela purchased mama's crib thirty-six years ago. A few kids play on the sidewalk in front of the store, three of them kicking a soccer ball back and forth next to a boy sitting on a stool, blowing bubbles. Beside him, a girl in a plaid dress ties up her hair and draws purple flowers with sidewalk chalk. Abuelo stops, puts his hands in his pockets, and shakes his head.

"What?" I say.

He tells me that kids these days are out of control. Back in his day, he says, it was not considered a bad thing to hit your kids. Growing up, everyone hit him. His parents, his aunts, his cousins. But then one day, after he raised mama, it was like someone decided it was wrong. And then things like this happened, he says, pointing to the kids.

"They're just playing," I say quietly to myself. In English so he cannot understand me.

He keeps walking. At the next block, he stops in front of a cake shop that he says only sells tres leches cakes and Mexican soda. I hear the buzz of the fridge through the open window.

Here, he hands me a white envelope. "This is for emergencies only," he tells me in Spanish. "Don't use it. Don't let your mom see, either." It feels thick, like a pad of felt.

I do not know what to do with it—it almost feels too big for my hands, too heavy. I stick it into my jacket pocket.

"Gracias," I say.

We get home ten minutes later. Mama asks where we went, and abuelo holds up the box of pastries.

"I'll put on a pot of coffee," she says, then turns toward the kitchen.

I go into the bedroom and close the door. I open the envelope. In twenties: three hundred dollars.

Abuelo tells mama to name what she wants—to name it and he will give it to her if it means we would stay. New clothes? New shoes? Tell me. Mama says she has already made up her mind and abuelo slams his fist on the kitchen counter so hard, the spatulas and whisks and knives shake in the drawer.

When we get to the new apartment, abuelo hugs us goodbye, wet puckered kisses on each of our foreheads. He tells us to call him anytime, hands me a folded note with his phone number. Already, I can see mama's smile becoming her own again. The puppet strings are cut, there, sprawled on the floor. Abuelo stoops down to kiss the top of Rafa's head, patting him on the back. "Bye, mijo," he says. "Bye, mija."

"Bye," I say.

We wave as he drives away in his car. I let out a breath when, in the distance, the blue of his pickup truck fades into the blue of the sky.

After he leaves, we walk up the stairs to our unit. The building looks like a three-tiered cake, the levels stacked right on top of each other, a white trim separating the layers like piped-on frosting. Even inside the building, the popcorn walls look like icing that still needs to be smoothed over with a spatula, bumpy beneath my fingertips. When the manager opens the door to our unit, Rafa and I rush into the bedroom that is the closest to the front door, the one mama says he and I will share.

In the corner of the room is a metal bunk bed with a ladder attached to the side, two blue mattresses leaning against the wall, a plastic-wrapped package of white bedsheets and towels on the table facing the window. Rafa says he will take the top bunk. I do not mind. I hold the ladder steady as he climbs it. It wobbles slightly.

"We'll have to fix that," I say, jiggling it.

Together, Rafa and I lift the mattresses and fit them into the bed frames while mama signs some paperwork in the living room. We pull the sheets over our beds, the pillowcases over the pillows, bringing them up to our noses to smell first. They smell a little like burnt rubber.

"Shouldn't we wash them first?" he asks me.

"I think it's okay."

While Rafa is distracted getting his T. rex to stand on top of the bedside table without falling over, I unzip the front pocket of my backpack and grab the white envelope, then stick it deep into my pillowcase. I think about the gift card. If it still had money on it, more than fifty cents, anyway, I would keep it right here too.

Mama's room looks the same as ours except that it is about half the size, the window by her bed unusually small, smaller than a library book. She will use the bottom bunk for storage, she says, clicking her pen closed, straightening out the paperwork.

She tells us to check the bathroom while she makes sure everything in the kitchen works. There are secondhand pots and pans in the cabinets, two spatulas and one knife in the drawers, a stack of mismatched paper plates and cups in the one near the sink. Rafa and I swing open the bathroom door. We twist the knob on the shower until water comes out cold, cold, then hot. Royal Melon goes on the rim of the tub in a caddy. I turn on the faucet in the bathroom sink—clear water. We go to the kitchen, where mama is standing in front of the stove, switching the oven light on and off.

"It works," she says, nodding, hands at her hips. Almost hesitant, she turns to face us. She clears her throat. "Do you want chicken for dinner tonight?"

And it sounds like a TV show. Like a family of four with a mom and a dad and a two-story house and they are deciding what to eat. Like they did every night, no big deal. To be asked a question like that. To say "yes"—it sounds like a line from a script. Like all we have to do is say it.

Rafa and I look at each other. "Sure," we say.

When we get home from the market, we watch as mama pats the chicken thighs dry with a paper towel and sprinkles them with salt and pepper. Rafa leans on the counter as she rinses off a few carrots, chopping them into thick orange coins. Then she cuts apples into cubes as small as dice. While I wash the cutting board with hot, soapy water, Rafa says we should gamble with the carrot coins and apple dice and wager something good, like dessert.

Mama says no. "No gambling."

The oven clanks as it heats, expanding. She makes a bed of carrots and apples on a glass tray and pours olive oil out in a zigzag drizzle and mixes them all up with her hands, until everything is glistening wet, the salt and pepper reflecting in the light like black-and-white glitter. She puts the chicken on top, covers the tray with foil, and pushes it into the oven, 375 degrees.

Twenty, twenty-five, thirty minutes.

At each interval, Rafa asks mama if it is done yet, tugging on her shirt. The place fills up with the smell of roasting, like abuelo's house on Christmas, something like warm salt, the coffee brewing.

Mama places a pan on the burner and turns it on high. A flame flutters underneath the frying pan like a twenty-winged blue-and-orange butterfly. After thirty seconds or so, she lowers it to medium. She uses oven mitts to take the tray out of the oven, removes the foil, and one by one, sears the chicken thighs on the pan. The chicken crisps in brown patches on contact, smoking. She cuts into one—white and juicy, dripping.

"Come eat," she says.

We sit on the floor, the three of us cross-legged on the carpet in the living room with our plates on our laps, napkins tucked underneath our thighs. Mama says she will ask management for a dining set tomorrow. In all of the excitement, none of us noticed they were missing. "There was a table and chairs in the pictures online," she says.

But for now, there is music. Faint music: knives scraping plates, hands crumpling napkins, chicken bones sucked dry. We are full-bellied when the song ends.

The next day, mama tells us she will be back in a few hours, grabs her keys, and closes the door without mentioning where she is going. It is the first time Rafa and I have had the house to ourselves. He sets up a card game on the floor.

"No cheating," I say as he shuffles the cards.

In the quiet, there is the light dripping of the sink, droplets splatting flat on the metal no matter how many paper towels we stuff into the faucet. The creaking of the bathroom door when a breeze nudges it open. The thudding footsteps from the neighbors upstairs. I boil water in a pot on the stove then pour it into two mugs, the chamomile tea bags expanding, puffy, the water turning yellow.

"Ready?" he asks, and takes the mug I hand him with both hands. "I'll go first."

After three rounds, me winning one, Rafa winning two, he walks toward the window, parts the curtains, and presses his hands to the glass. I can tell what he is thinking.

"We should go outside," he says. "To the park."

"I don't think so."

"What? It's not like we have to tell her."

"I don't have keys. I wouldn't be able to lock the apartment. Or get in through the front gate."

"We won't be gone that long. Come on," he says. "Please."

I sigh. The park is a few blocks away. It would take us ten minutes to get there and mama said she would be gone for a few hours. "Let me think."

I walk to our room, pull the white envelope out from under my pillow, and grab a twenty-dollar bill. I fold it in half and stick it in my pocket.

"Okay," I say back in the living room, glancing at the clock. "Just this once." I look out the window: a pasty white sky, the color of glue. "Grab us an umbrella, okay?"

"I don't think we have one."

Downstairs, I tell Rafa to bring a rock from the parking lot while I hold the gate open with my foot. He hands me a smooth reddish-brown stone.

"Thanks."

I place it by the base of the gate to keep it from closing. We walk three and a half blocks to the park, making sure to look both ways before crossing the street. It starts to sprinkle. A few minutes later rain collects on the corner of my eyebrow, then drops onto my cheek. I wipe my face with the sleeve of my sweater. When we get to the park, there is something musty in the air, peppery, the smell of wet wood, and I look around at the rain soaking into the park benches, the picnic tables, the wood chips at the base of each tree. In the middle of the park, by the gazebo, stands an ice cream cart under a red-and-white pinwheel umbrella, rain bouncing off it like a trampoline.

Rafa looks at me. We walk over.

I read through the menu, a chalkboard sign, the words drooping, distorted in the rain. They only have flavors I have never heard of. Honey Truffle Espresso, Bergamot, Cherry Rum, Paprika. "Buster's Experimental Scoops and Drinks," reads a metal sign attached to the base of the cart.

When I hear someone get in line behind us, I turn around. A man in a blue poncho.

"You can go ahead," I say to him. "Still deciding."

I read the flavors aloud to Rafa, who scrunches his nose and shakes his head, then turn to look at the drink menu: water, coffee, and hot chocolate with a large red asterisk.

"They have hot chocolate," I say to Rafa, and follow the asterisk to the bottom of the sign. "But it has chili oil in it."

I step closer to the ice cream cart after the man in front of me orders. "Excuse me, do you have rainbow?"

"Rainbow?" the cashier says.

"The flavor."

"We do not."

We walk toward the front of the park again, where the wind has picked up, piling brown leaves together at the base of a slide like an invisible rake.

"Can I?" Rafa asks.

I nod. "Careful, though. Might be slippery."

Rafa climbs the ladder, pushes himself down the slide, and lands feet-first in the pile of leaves. The man in the poncho is sitting alone, sipping from a coffee cup. He checks his watch, rests an elbow on the picnic table, and looks at the playground. It starts to rain harder, the wind pushing my hair back as if I am standing in front of a fan.

"We should get back," I say after Rafa's third time down the slide. "Don't want you to get sick."

The man leaves the park when we do. For a block, he walks a few paces behind us, and when he is still there a block later, his shadow stretching toward us, about to overlap with mine on the sidewalk, I hold Rafa closer to me. I turn around. The poncho is pulled over his face, down to his nose. Is he following us? If he follows us all the way back to our apartment, I do not know what I would do, what I would grab. A knife, maybe. Yes, a kitchen knife, I nod to myself.

Just then, a phone rings.

"Hi, honey," he says brightly. "Sorry I'm late. Yes, I'm walking there right now. I'm right around the corner." He turns right, then walks into a restaurant with a lemon tree in a pot by the entrance. We keep walking. I soften my grip on Rafa.

When we return to the apartment building, I remove the rock from the foot of the gate then walk up the stairs to our unit. I breathe out. Everything is exactly as we left it: the cards on the floor, the mugs in the sink, the box of tea on the counter. I place the twenty-dollar bill back under my pillow, then lie down on my bed, staring up through the slats to the mattress above. I am so relieved I could cry. After a few minutes, I walk back into the living room.

"Another round of cards?" I say.

A couple of hours later mama arrives with two shopping bags, one in each hand, grabs a roll of tape from a drawer in the kitchen, then disappears into her bedroom.

"Do you want your real Christmas presents now? Even though it's New Year's," mama asks after dinner, vegetable stir-fry over rice. Rafa jumps up and down, squealing. "Sorry they were late this year."

She hands us two boxes wrapped in lipstick-red paper, a silky white ribbon tied into a loose knot on top. Unwrapped, they are a set of acrylic paint tubes and flat-bristle paintbrushes for me; for Rafa, a box of dinosaur eggs and a winding racetrack for his toy cars. I open the box of paint, run my fingertips along the ridges of the caps—titanium white, jet black, cadmium yellow medium hue, cadmium red, cobalt blue. I can paint decorations for the apartment. A seahorse peeking out of a curtain of kelp. A rowboat riding a spiraled wave. Rafa runs up to mama and hugs her.

"Can I use one now?" he says, pulling away.

We fill the bathtub with warm water and drop a dinosaur egg inside, watching the muddy clay dissolve until a brontosaurus action figure emerges, brown and grimy. He shakes the water off it and dries it with a towel. Afterward, we make chocolate cake from a box, cracking eggs into the bowl and picking out the small white shell breakings that fall in. I help Rafa whisk the eggs until the yolks are runny. Fingers licked clean, we sit by the oven and watch the cake puff and rise.

When the timer goes off, Rafa shouts, "Happy New Year!"

"Happy New Year's," mama and I say back, the three of us smiling with the cake, the dinosaurs, the paint, the brushes, and the chirping of the timer. After the cake cools, we stick a candle in the middle and then light it, the flame an orange tongue licking the air, flickering.

"Here," she says later, handing me another present.

"What is it?" I ask.

I open it. A lilac journal with a lock on it. She hands me the key. I reach over to hug her.

On Monday, a man wearing a gray baseball cap backward knocks on our door and introduces himself, the pull-strap tight across his forehead. He says he is one of the groundskeepers on staff here and his name is Lucas. Management told him he has to install a sign inside of our apartment.

"A sign?" mama asks.

"Yes, ma'am."

She lets him in. He scrapes the bottom of his shoes on the doormat outside before walking inside, and chunks of dirt come loose, landing around the mat in grass-speckled clumps. I know mama will ask me to sweep it up later.

"Should be quick," he says, and sets his toolbox down on the floor in a grunt.

After a few minutes of drilling, wall shavings landing in a small white pile, there is a list of rules plastered on the front-facing wall of the living room, a sign bolted down with black knobby screws on each of its four corners. Lucas tells us to read it over and that if we cannot understand any part of it, to ask Juan, the gardener, out back and he will translate it into Spanish for us.

"You already read them over when you signed your lease and, of course, are doing the things you're supposed to, but management just wanted everyone to have a copy of them inside the apartment," he says, and closes the door behind him. "Oh, and we'll look for a dining set for you guys tomorrow. Sorry about that."

Mama and I read the rules. We have a curfew of ten thirty p.m. on weekdays and eleven thirty p.m. on weekends. If we want to leave the complex after curfew, we have to ask Lucas at the front desk for permission two nights before so that he can plan ahead to open the gate. Mama has to attend on-site parenting and financial literacy classes as well as babysit some of the other residents' children twice a week so that they can attend parenting classes too. We have to participate in fire drills in order to know the safety procedures in the event of a real fire. We have to pay our rent on time, even though it is reduced rent, or face eviction. Drug testing is every other week on a day and time of the supervisor's choosing. We cannot smoke or drink on the property. Noise should be kept to a minimum at all times. Signed, Greater Care Shelter.

"Sometimes in the money class," mama tells me a few days later as she chops a tomato, "they ask me a question, and I pretend I don't speak English."

I laugh and add the onions to the pan. "Mama, sometimes when you tell me to wash the dishes, I pretend I don't understand your Spanish."

"You a doctor?" a man sitting on a folding chair a door down from ours asks, setting a glass cup on a green patio table. An amber-colored liquid sloshes around inside the glass. We have just gotten home from the market.

"Not a doctor. A nurse." Mama digs through her purse for her keys.

"Figured that was a costume or something," he says, pointing at mama, her scrubs. "But then I saw you at the clinic. Twisted my ankle yesterday." He lifts a gauze-wrapped foot out of his sandal.

"A costume?" mama repeats.

He shrugs. "You never know. People do all kinds of things these days," he says, then looks at us. "Well, hello there." He hobbles over to us on one foot. "I'm your neighbor. Arthur." Supporting himself on the wall, he reaches out his hand. Mama shakes it, then me, then Rafa.

"Hi, Arthur," mama says.

"Art's fine," he says. "And your names are?"

"Nina." She pulls her key chain out of her bag and then puts it in her pocket.

"Sofia."

"Rafa."

"Nice to meet you," he says, and hops back to his seat. "You know, you being a nurse and all, I was wondering if I could ask you something. Don't want to take up too much of your time, but the doctor said something I didn't quite catch. My hearing's not the best." He tugs on his ear. "I think he said something about rice. Now, am I to understand that he wants me to eat rice, or to put my foot in rice? I went out and bought a bag after my appointment, but I don't know what to do with it."

"Rice?" mama says, confused. "Oh, you mean R.I.C.E. Rest, Ice, Compression, Elevation."

The man considers this. "That makes a lot more sense." He takes a sip from his glass. "Well, I guess I have to go buy an ice tray."

"We have ice," Rafa says.

"I'll bring you some," mama says. "Just give me a few minutes."

"That's very kind of you. I'd appreciate that."

Mama lets us inside and tells us to start putting the groceries away. She opens the freezer, fills a small plastic bag full of ice, presses it closed, and walks outside, where she stands with him for half an hour, talking about his foot, a gash on his big toe, the skin yellowing around it, before she comes inside.

"That was nice of you," I say.

She shrugs. "It's nice to help."

Early the next morning, an hour before mama has to leave for work, she opens our door to a woman in a blue sundress and leather sandals. "Nina? Does a Nina live here?" the woman asks, holding a newborn baby to her chest.

My heart drops. But it is not the girl—this lady is blond, a few years older, the voice high-pitched, completely different.

"I am so sorry to bother you," she says through the screen

door. “But I heard you were a doctor.” The baby is screaming, tiny pink fists punching the air.

“Nurse,” Rafa corrects her. He pours himself a bowl of cereal in the kitchen.

“A nurse, I’m sorry,” the woman says, rocking the baby in her arms. “I just had him two weeks ago. And there’s this rash. I just noticed it,” she says, pulling the onesie down his neck.

“Let me see,” mama says, opens the door, and lifts the baby from her arms.

By the end of the week, at least ten people have stopped by, an older couple with the same wiry white hair, a woman with toddler triplets, a dad and his teenage daughter. The dad, a man in his fifties who only spoke Spanish, was so grateful to mama for her help, he asked his wife to crochet her a winter hat, even though she has arthritis.

“What’s your favorite color?” he asked mama as he was leaving.

“Green,” mama said, gently closing the screen door.

The next day, a green beanie with a salmon-colored bobble shaped like a flower appeared in our mailbox. It sits like a lily pad on the kitchen counter. After she sees the last of them, she collapses on the couch, lets out a deep sigh, and asks me to lock the door. She looks tired but happy, her hand on her forehead. Later I hear her humming to herself.

Brushing our teeth in the bathroom, the spearmint toothpaste foaming up white in our mouths, I ask if a friend can visit.

"She's nice. She's in my class," I say, rinsing out my mouth.

"What's her name?"

"Ana."

Mama thinks about it. "When? Not tomorrow. I have work tomorrow."

"Maybe later this week, then."

"How about Saturday?"

I call Ana using the house phone and tell her that she should come over if she wants to, that my mom says she can. She says this sounds fun—she is stuck at the Boys & Girls Club all day on Saturday anyway, doing nothing, and she could probably walk over here, since it is so close by. She says that Antonio hangs out there too. "I really think he likes me," she says, whispering.

With one hand over the receiver, I motion to mama to get her attention and then ask if two friends can come over instead of one.

She raises her eyebrows. "I didn't know you were so popular," she says. "Sure."

I tell Ana to bring him too.

Ana and Antonio come over on Saturday to eat pozole with us, which mama wakes up at eight thirty in the morning to make. The three of us come up with routes that swerve around the complex so we can avoid our classmates who volunteer here on the weekends with their families for extra credit in religion class. Ana and Antonio want to get from here to there, back around this way, cutting through the community garden, and I sketch out the shortest way based on distances and triangles, like Pythagoras. The two of them look at each other. "She's smart," they whisper, like it is personal and serious and urgent.

We sit at a table near the front of the complex, dry patches of grass like bald spots on the lawn, and talk about Ms. Clyde until noon. The way she says "fractions" like "frictions" and the way she puts the three of us together, mixes up our names at recess. Antonio scoots his chair closer to us. He says that people like us have to stick together. Ana says that he probably just heard that from a movie, and he leans back and crosses his arms and says he probably did but that it does not make it any less true.

Antonio points to me. "I didn't even know you were Mexican when I saw you. Only when Ana told me."

I look down, brushing a piece of lint off my jeans as I think of what to say.

"I mean, you look," he says, searching for something, "I don't know. I just couldn't tell."

"Yeah, me neither," says Ana. "I could tell by looking at your eyes, maybe. But it doesn't really matter."

"It's like, I couldn't figure out what you were," Antonio says.

"I'm only half Mexican," I say. "Maybe that's why."

"Really?"

"Yeah."

They both look at me, trying to make it seem like they are not. I see it from the corner of my eye. Just a casual glance this way. Ana looks at my eyebrows and Antonio scans lower, maybe my lips. I readjust myself in my chair. I wonder if there is something on my face, in my teeth, a cilantro leaf, maybe, or a flake of black pepper. I cover my mouth with my hand and run my tongue over my teeth to be sure. Nothing dislodges. In a way, it would be better if there were something in there.

"Well, what else are you?" Antonio asks.

"Egyptian," I say.

"That's cool." He nods.

"Yeah," Ana says. "That's cool."

The way they are looking at me, it is like they are deciding whether or not my eyes are Egyptian, if my nose is Mexican, who my skin color belongs to, dividing me up like that, ears, lips, forehead. I want them to stop looking at me, to change the subject, but I do not know what to say, what to do. I remember the sixth-and-seventh-grade field trip Ms. Clyde mentioned before break. "So, the zoo—" I start.

"Do you know Egyptian?" Antonio asks.

Ana smacks his shoulder. "Arabic, menso. It's called Arabic."

I nod. "A little bit. I don't know it perfectly."

"So, like your Spanish?" he asks.

I look down. "I guess so."

"Does that mean you know hieroglyphics?"

"My god, Antonio," Ana says. "Leave her alone."

"Okay, okay, I'm sorry," he says, his hands up by his face.

Then mama walks downstairs and tells us to come inside. She says that the pozole is ready, wiping her hands dry on the skirt of her apron. "Come, wash your hands," she says. We follow her up the outside stairs. Our footsteps reverberate on the metal, the entire spiral of the staircase shaking.

I could tell them what baba told me, that we come from pharaohs. One time, I asked him which ones, and he just said, "Pharaohs, habibti."

"I know," I said. "But their names."

"I don't know their names," he said, and threw his hands in the air like the question was ridiculous, unfair. I wanted to be able to tell my friends at school that I came from pharaoh so-and-so. I could point to something in a museum and say, Don't we look alike?

"Then how can you know we're related to them?" I said carefully. "If you don't know their names, I mean."

And he said, "Don't challenge me, Sofia. It's not nice."

"Thank you for letting us come over," Ana says now, setting her backpack on the floor. "It smells so good."

"Of course," mama says. "I hope you like it."

Mama gets out five bowls and ladles pozole into each, scraping up extra chicken from the bottom of the pot. She pours broth over the hominy, and the steam rises up into my nose as I breathe it in, sharp and hot. I carry the bowls to the dining table, which mama bargained for at the thrift shop before it closed yesterday. Management said they could not find a spare dining set. The owner of the thrift shop threw in an extra chair—tan wood with pink and blue flowers painted on it—for free. He said he liked mama's confidence. He leaned in close to her and said that if she ever needed anything, even if it was at night, to call him on the number listed on his business card, which she spat her gum into and folded up when we got back to the car. She chops up onion and cilantro and limes for us to put into the soup and sets them on the table in small bowls.

"Mm," Antonio says, throwing his head back. "It tastes just like how my tía makes it."

"It's really good," I say, looking across the dining room to her, and she smiles, lowering the flame on the stove to a flutter. Rafa sits across from me, small among us older kids, squeezing a lime wedge over his bowl with both hands, struggling.

I take it and squeeze it for him over his bowl, the light green juice landing on top of the red broth.

"Thanks," he says. He picks up his spoon.

"You're so lucky you get to eat like this all the time," Antonio says. "My mom never cooks. Maybe your mom could teach her."

"What about your dad?" Ana asks him. "Mine loves to cook. Has his own apron and everything."

"He doesn't cook either," Antonio says. "Does your dad live here too?"

Mama stops mid-step. "No," I say, the mention of baba like a paper cut on my skin, small but there. Up until now, this space was only for the three of us, and now it is like baba is in the room, the lemon in his cologne blowing through the open windows, the way he clears his throat, here, echoing in the dining room. "We just moved here."

"Oh," he says, and looks at my mom, then me. "To me, you look more like your mom. More Mexican. But maybe you look like your dad too." He pats my thigh, and I pull my leg back, a red patch of unexpected warmth sprouting where he touched me, like he scalded me but not in a bad way. It radiates down to my toes, the rush of it.

"Yeah," I say, crossing my left leg over my right. "Maybe."

That night, washing my face, I can conjure Antonio without trying—his scent, cinnamon, nutmeg—and I can think of what he looks like with and without glasses, how they frame his face, what the indents on either side of his nose look like when he removes them, two small pinches. Reaching for the towel, I remember that he had used it earlier today, that his own hands had touched it. I bring it up to my nose, wondering if his scent has somehow knitted itself into the fabric. I drape it over the towel rack, disappointed. It smells like Royal Melon.

"What's with you?" mama asks me, nudging my side while I am standing over the sink in the kitchen a few minutes later, pouring myself a glass of water.

"What?" I ask, smiling.

"That," she says, pointing to my face.

"It's nothing," I say.

"Nothing? That's funny," she says. "I thought his name was Antonio." She smiles. Then her face falls, like she has dropped it, her smile, somewhere on the kitchen floor. "Careful, though," she says, placing her hand on the counter. "Boys can complicate things."

The night before we return to school mama tells us to put on nice clothes. "We're going out to eat," she says. "I just got my paycheck."

Rafa wears his beige school uniform pants and a button-down shirt, rolling up his sleeves so they sit at his wrists. Mama and I wear dresses we never wore when we were in the car. Mine is flowy and magenta with three white buttons down the middle, and hers, navy blue with a thin belt. We had worn them to my birthday party in October. When I zip mine up, I notice the dress feels tight across my chest but also strangely loose around my waist. I feel the fabric shift when I breathe.

She drives us to an Italian restaurant up a few blocks from the highway. We order lemonade for the table, and I like the sound of that—"for the table." There are forks and knives tucked into cloth napkins, a lazy Susan that Rafa spins until mama tells him to stop, people are looking. When the food arrives—garlic bread and calamari and spaghetti with meat sauce—the lazy Susan goes around and around for the rest of the night, spinning out its own circumference.

"Want some bread?" mama asks, holding the basket out in front of me.

"Sure." I take a piece from the middle of the loaf. It is spongy and warm.

Mama pours olive oil into a shallow bowl, drops a dot of balsamic vinegar in the middle, and places it in front of me. Antonio has eyes like this: a pale pool shimmering around a dark droplet. My side aches. I dip the bread inside, ruining the eye.

Last year, Lena would see Johnny, a sixth grader she had a crush on, everywhere we went, even if he was not there. Like he was a ghost, like she was haunted. One time, after PE class, Lena laid her head down on her desk, saying she felt sick after brushing hands with him for a second in capture the flag. "It's called butterflies," Chloe said, smoothing Lena's hair back.

"I know what butterflies are," Lena said, then groaned. She said she felt so sick, she was considering going to the school nurse's office, or even going home. It was strange watching her act like this because of Johnny, who always picked his nose in science class and then wiped it on his pants, and who mama called Mr. Tumble because of how often he tripped over his own laces during junior varsity volleyball practice. But now I feel butterflies—sharp moths—with their needles-for-legs, their box-cutter wings, landing inside my rib cage, then taking off.

After we finish dinner, mama asks for the bill. She leaves a tip, signing her name on the bottom of the receipt with an extra flair, like someone asked for her autograph.

"Now," she says, putting her credit card back in her wallet. "I have a very important question for you."

Rafa and I look up from our plates.

"Want ice cream?"

Lately, I pinch the soft plushiness that has appeared around my hips, as if someone has stuffed a teddy bear with more fluff around its thighs and backside and chest—a tad more here, some around there, enough for me to notice when I look at a mirror. Mama says I am becoming grown. That this is a good thing. But I want it off, and sometimes, standing by the mirror in the bathroom, I try to pinch it off, pinching the extra skin until it turns red.

Other things she said have come true. Hair sprouts like brown weeds under my arms, sweat stains turn yellow, my feet smell sour when I take off my shoes. When I tell her, she looks up from her newspaper. "Have you started your period yet?"

"Not yet," I say.

She nods, takes a sip of coffee, then sets the cup down on the table.

"Why?"

"We just have to get some stuff before it happens," she says, explaining to me about the pads, the ibuprofen, the stain remover, the heating pads, the raspberry leaf tea.

"Heating pads?" I ask. "Isn't it too warm out?"

"They're for cramps," she says, pointing to her stomach.

"Cramps?" Even the word sounds like it hurts. My stomach sinks low, low, and I wonder if this is what a cramp feels like.

We are sitting at the table the next morning eating breakfast when I let out a big yawn.

"Sleep okay?" mama asks, pouring herself a dark trickle of coffee.

I yawn wider, covering my mouth, and nod. "Just tired."

For two nights now, I have woken up in a panic at midnight to double-check that the money abuelo gave me is still under my pillow, sliding my hand underneath until I felt the sharp edge of the envelope. Both nights, I had a hard time falling back asleep.

Mama clears her throat, then clears it again until Rafa and I look up at her.

"So, sex," she says. "Don't do it."

I almost spit out my tea. "What?"

"Okay?" she says, leaning forward, her hands flat on the table.

Rafa and I nod. As she continues on, we nod some more to try and make it stop. Before we finish our toast, there are suddenly penises and vaginas underneath our clothes and the word "pregnant" swirling in the heat above the coffee. She puts her purse on the table and unzips it, pulling out a pocket-size full-color encyclopedia.

"What's that?" Rafa asks.

She ignores him. "Listen, no storks, no 'special delivery.' None of that. Look," she says, nudging me. "You too," she tells Rafa. "This is what it takes to make a baby."

Mama points to the diagrams, to the naked woman and man and their hairy pink organs, and explains what is what—what the nine months are like, that it is really ten months if you think about it, because nine times four is only thirty-six and pregnancy can last forty weeks, sometimes more, and that ten months is a long time, that the eighteen years until they are fully grown is an even longer time, not to mention the cost of it all, and kids cost so much, you two cost so much, do you know that?

"Promise me, no kids for a long time," she says, closing the encyclopedia.

I promise, hot-cheeked and uncomfortable. But Rafa, it seems, could not care less. He is distracted by the clacking of the blinds against the open window.

"Rafa," mama says. "You promise?"

"Yeah, sure," he says.

I shift in my seat. My cheeks, I imagine, are seared red as it starts to make sense. One day at the house, when I stayed home from school because I had a fever, I saw the girl with baba in the living room. It was after mama left to run an errand, after she pressed the back of her hand to my forehead and told me I probably caught something from one of the kids at school. She said there was a can of chicken noodle soup in the pantry that I could heat up when I got hungry, that the can opener was in the utensil drawer, next to the vegetable peeler, and she would be back in the afternoon.

"Get some rest, okay?" she said. "I'll leave baba a note."

After I fell back asleep, I woke up, startled, to a loud, piercing cry. It sounded like a wailing cat, like someone was repeatedly stepping on its tail. I pulled myself out of bed, my head foggy, slow. I grabbed whatever I could find, whatever was closest to me. Rafa's action figure with real metal spikes for claws. I ran into the hallway, then stopped, listened. The cries sounded like they were coming from a person. A woman, maybe. The girl. I ran back into Rafa's room and grabbed a towel from his closet, because what if she was giving birth? In the movies, when that happens, somebody always asks for a towel. Towel in my left hand, action figure in my right, I ran into the living room.

Baba was supposed to be at work, so when I saw him there behind her, I felt relieved: He could help her and I could go back to bed. They were both facing the wall. I stood in the hallway while the sounds got louder and louder, baba holding on to the girl, his grasp desperate. I did not know what to do. I was stunned. I walked back to my room, my face hot, trying to figure out a way to let them know I was home without telling them. I reached my hand out to knock over the lamp on the nightstand—it was made of plastic, so I knew it would not break but still crash loudly enough for them to hear.

"Sorry!" I called out after the crash. "Don't worry. I'm fine."

A minute later, after the jangling of belt buckles and the click of button snaps, baba knocked on the door and walked in. "I didn't know you were here."

My eyes, averted, were full of knowing, even if I tried to make them look like they were not, blinking it away. "Mama left you a note on the counter."

"A note?"

"I'm sick."

Baba backed away a step, as I expected him to. He hated

germs, would hold his breath and walk into his office whenever Rafa and I coughed or sneezed, even if it was from allergies. "Do you need anything?" he asked from the doorframe.

I shook my head, bringing the blanket up to my chin.

"I'll make you some tea."

When he returned, it was with a glass mug, tea spilling onto the saucer with each step. He set it down on the bedside table. I could see the mint leaves settling, a pool of honey at the bottom. He handed me a spoon. I took a sip. It scalded my tongue.

Tossing and turning in bed a few minutes later, unable to sleep, I walked out to use the bathroom and found them sitting together on the couch, watching TV with his arm around her. Their laughs were harmonized, a low note and high note played at the same time on a piano. After a minute or so, I was about to turn back to my room, but just then, the girl moved her hand across his lap, picked up the remote, and muted the show. The characters' mouths still moved on the screen. "Can I ask you something?" she said.

Baba nodded.

"Do you think they'll call me 'Mom' one day?"

His smile dropped. "Who, the kids?"

"Of course the kids. Who else?"

He cleared his throat and moved his arm back down to his side. His face grew shadowed, like there was once sunlight but a cloud passed overhead. "All right, I have to go to work," he said, lifting himself off the couch.

"Wait, I asked you a question," she said as he got up. "Hey," she said when he did not answer. "I love you, okay? I love you."

He kissed her cheek. I blinked. When he locked the door behind him, she stood there, facing it. She lifted her hand to her face, touching the spot where he had kissed. Then she began to cry, leaning her head against the door.

"I know you're there," she said, sniffling. "I can hear you breathing."

I expected her to turn around and face me, to tell me to leave, or maybe ask me to stay, but she just stood there, staring at the door. I walked back to my room, lowered myself into bed, then pulled the covers over my head. When I woke up a few hours later, it was to mama tapping my shoulder, asking why the can of chicken soup was still in the cabinet. I told her I forgot about it.

Mama says we have to laugh about things sometimes. She laughs now, bent over the kitchen counter, her fingers wrapped around the neck of a spray bottle. Inside, vinegar, water, and blue dish soap slosh together, a web of bubbles on top of the cloudy water.

"There!" Rafa says, pointing to the wall.

She turns around and aims the spray bottle at three black bugs clustered like freckles. Two of them slide down the wall, wriggling until they stop moving, suspended in water droplets. The other one has fled, flown up to the ceiling.

"Damn it," she says, laughing with her arm over her stomach, almost falling to the floor. "This is ridiculous."

Over the past week small bugs have begun to appear around our apartment. We thought they were moths. They fluttered around the kitchen with their spotted wings. At night, with all the lights turned off, we lit candles and waited for them to fly over to us. One of them singed a wing in the flame then flew toward the window, a small wisp of smoke trailing behind it. It landed on the windowpane. The rest we cupped in our hands to release outside.

But the next day, there were even more.

We tried everything: smashing them flat with napkins, spraying them with disinfectant until it ran out and we had to make our own using things we had at home.

At first they only hovered near the kitchen sink, on the wall directly behind the faucet. They did not bother us, did not bite or sting, but mama said we needed them gone, that the housing manager would be unhappy if she were to find out, thinking we brought them with us. We took shifts. I sprayed them in the morning. Rafa, after school, while mama made dinner. He made a game of it. He kept track of how many he got, piling them in his hand after, their little legs pointed straight up in the air.

Yesterday, when I walked into the bathroom to shower, six of them perched on my knee, landing two at a time. I shooed them away, then pulled the shower curtain back and saw the tub dotted with them, like someone had thrown a handful of black sesame seeds into the tub. "Look," I said, pulling mama into the bathroom. "They're in here too."

"Shit," she said, bending down at the foot of the tub to get a closer look.

In the evening, she boiled a pot of water to make oatmeal for dinner. Just as she poured the packet of oats into the pot, one of the bugs dove in and she cursed, its body melting like a black inkblot in the oatmeal. I imagined biting into it, the crunch of the wings, the thin snap of the legs.

She turned off the stove. "Stupid bug," she said, pouring out the oatmeal into the trash. I frowned. The oatmeal was strawberries and cream. My favorite.

Tonight, when we go to the library, I look them up on the

computer, wincing at the screen, at the close-up pictures of their wriggly ribbed larvae. "Found them," I say, calling mama over from the magazine aisle. "They're not moths. They're called 'drain flies.'" I click on an article. "Also called 'sewer flies.'"

She scrunches up her nose.

Rafa makes a fake throw-up sound. "Gross."

"How do we get rid of them?" she asks, leaning closer to the screen.

"We need to pour baking soda and vinegar down all of the drains," I say. "And if that doesn't work, bleach. And if even that doesn't work," I say, scrolling, "then there's this orange stuff we can buy, but it's expensive."

"How much?"

"Sixty," I say. "Plus shipping."

The article says that when they hatch, they feast on the soap suds and hair, on anything caught in the drains. "It says they're mostly around in the summer. I don't know why we're getting them now."

"It's been humid," she says.

We pick up two boxes of baking soda at the market, and when we get home, we pour it down all of the drains in the house—kitchen sink, bathroom sink, shower—packing in the ash-white powder. We let the drains sit overnight, then pour vinegar down them in the morning. The bubbles hiss as they seep up through the drain and into the tub.

"I think this will work," mama says, peering down into the drain with a flashlight. "We'll do this for a few days, then we can act like this never happened."

I nod, stumbling out of the bathroom, covering my mouth. I steady myself on a dining room chair. I feel nauseous, imagining the flies boiling alive in there, overwhelmed by the sharp smell of the vinegar, acidified, the eggs bursting open, larvae writhing, dissolving into goopy white sticky puddles. I want to splash cold water on my face, but mama says we should let the drains sit for a while before using them.

The next day, the phone rings as we are clearing the dinner table.

"One second," mama says after she answers, one hand covering the receiver. I am rinsing the last of the dishes, shaking water off a handful of forks before setting them down on the drying rack. "Sofia," she says, "Ana's mom is asking if you want to come over to her house tomorrow."

"Oh," I say, turning off the sink. "Can I?"

"Well, do you want to?"

Drying my hands with the kitchen towel, I think of what I would wear, if Ana would notice me wearing the same shirt I wore when she came over, if that would matter to her. And what would I bring, my backpack? Homework? "Sure," I say, feeling unsure.

When Ana's dad pulls his car, silver as a spoon, up to the curb in front of our unit the next day, he waves at us, and mama waves back, saying, "Thank you! Have fun!" loud enough for him to hear. "We will!" he says back, and I notice his voice is not as deep as baba's, a little lighter, gentler. Walking to his car, I try to take in Greater Care as he would—the white stacked buildings, the red flowers as small as raspberries near the main office, the bulletin board overflowing with sun-bleached flyers. I am relieved he is not coming inside our apartment. There are still a few drain fly bodies in the bathroom.

"Come," Ana says, her black hair spilling out the window. I open the car door.

"Sofia, hi," Ana's mom says when I walk in through the front door of their house, two-story and yellow with a stone path leading up to it. There are orange flowers spread out like palms on both sides of the path. She opens her arms wide for a hug. "I'm Juana, Ana's mom. Please," she says, motioning with her hand. "Come in. This is Olivia, and this is Mia." She rests her hands on top of the girls' heads as she says their names. They look about five or six. Ana calls them the Evil Twins. "Say hi to Sofia."

"Hi," they say shyly, Mia moving to hide behind her mom's legs. Then Olivia, a braid ending in a sparkly purple hair tie, asks me, "Are you smart? Ana says you're smart."

"Shush, Olivia, you're so annoying," Ana says, covering her sister's mouth with her hand and pushing her behind the kitchen island. "Mami, we're going up to my room."

"Yeah, mami, we're going to Ana's room," Olivia says, pulling Mia by the rubber band she has on her wrist.

"No," Ana says. "Alone."

"But, mami—"

"Hey, niñas, let them be," Ana's mom says to the girls. Then to us, she says, "I'll call you two when dinner's ready, okay?"

The girls start to cry. First Mia, then Olivia.

I follow Ana to the top of the stairs, where she turns a corner. We walk inside her room—light lavender walls, a sheep-skin rug at the foot of her bed, a rectangular mirror by her closet, a picture frame of her family on her desk, the five of them on top of a mountain, each of them holding a plastic water bottle. The six or so round white feathery pillows on her bed look like a flock of geese crouched together. With her back turned, I run my fingers over her things: the alarm clock on her bedside table, the marbled dresser, a lamp humming warm light across the desk.

Above her desk: a bulletin board with feathers and buttons and fabric samples, strips of denim, paper-thin purple tulle, and silk folded into a triangle, then pinned to the bottom of the board.

Here, she reaches beneath her bed and pulls out a black composition book with "Science" written on the front in capital letters. "It's not really a science journal. It's my diary," she whispers. She touches the glittery bookmark wedged inside and then hands me the journal and tells me to read it.

"You want me to read it?"

"Why not? Friends can read each other's journals. It's practically their job."

I shake my head. "It's okay," I say, handing it back to her. I think of my journal at home, under my pillow. If I read her journal, she might ask to read mine.

She opens the journal to the bookmarked page, sets it on my lap, and points to the bottom. In all capital letters, it says, "Antonio kissed me." I look up. She is smiling, playing with the tips of her hair. She says she thinks she loves him. "I'm gonna tell him at the field trip on Wednesday. By the flamingos."

"I was worried at first," she says, her face flushing, her neck, even her arms. "I thought he liked you. But then I asked him, and he said no." She smiles. "And then he kissed me again."

I blink two, three times in a row, trying to stop seeing it, Antonio's lips slightly open, parted like a clam. His eyes closed.

"Nice," I manage to say.

I turn around and face the bulletin board, pretending to be interested in the fabric, my back toward Ana. I unpin the silk triangle and hand it to her. "This one's pretty."

After dinner—tostadas with ground beef and beans and sour cream—Ana and her sisters want to watch TV. When Roberto walks into the living room to hand us a tray of orange slices, he steps on the plastic arm of a Barbie doll and it snaps off, a severed white hand with small pink fingernails landing next to his foot on the hardwood floor. I hold my breath, waiting for it, for him to yell. He is right next to me, so it would be loud. Right in my ear.

"Well, that hurt," he says, rubbing the arch of his foot.

The girls glance up, then go back to playing, but I am still holding my breath, waiting for it. Roberto stumbles toward the couch. Ana's mom turns to Olivia and Mia and tells them to be careful with where they put their toys.

"Let me see," she says, patting the empty spot next to her on the couch. He sits down, sinking into the beige cushions, which flatten underneath him. "Pobrecito," she says, frowning slightly, bending down to look.

The way they are with each other, it is like they are friends. They listen to each other. Not like mama and baba, who ignore each other or interrupt each other when they tell stories from their past, shaking their heads and saying things like "That would never have happened" or accusing the other of exaggerating. Juana kisses Roberto's shoulder, then rises up to get an ice pack for his foot.

If Rafa had spilled orange juice on Roberto's work papers, I bet all Roberto would have done would be to stand up and get a roll of paper towels and dab it gently on the papers until they soaked up the juice. I bet the worst thing he has done—ever, ever done—is raise his voice.

Later, when Ana's dad drops me off, it is around nine at night. Ana has fallen asleep in the back seat, her head resting against the window, bobbing in time with the bumps in the road. Neon signs blur past us, the orange outline of a beer bottle surrounded by flashing pink hearts. A man wearing a black suit and a woman in a peach-colored dress cross the street in front of us, holding hands, smiling shyly, and I wonder if mama and baba ever looked like that, a little too sweet, dressed up for each other. I shake my head. I cannot imagine it. I hear the click of the turn signal.

"Mija?" Ana's dad says as he pulls up to the curb where he picked me up earlier.

I realize he is talking to me. "Sí?"

"Ana's still asleep?"

"Yes," I say, double-checking.

"Good. Listen. You know, she told me about the score you got on that test a while back. And about, well, all of your other scores. Do me a favor?" He turns to face me. The left side of his face is in a broad black shadow. "Will you help Ana stay on track at school? Her mom and I, we really want her to do well. I mean, she was doing well up until a few weeks ago. Straight A's. We don't know why they've dropped."

I think of Antonio.

"But it's useless coming from us. From you, though, from a friend, she might actually listen."

"I'll try," I say, smiling, a little embarrassed.

"Good. Tell your mom that you're welcome anytime, okay?"

"Well, *somebody* liked you," Ana says as she takes her seat next to me in class. "I could hardly hear the end of it when I got home last night. Here," she says, handing me a brown lunch bag with my name written on it. "He packed you a lunch. He woke up early to make it. Even sliced the strawberries into hearts and it's not even Valentine's Day."

I laugh. "That's so nice of him. Tell him that I say thank you." I peer into the bag. Chips, an apple, a sandwich, and a plastic container full of strawberries.

"Get used to it," she says, smiling. "You're basically one of us now."

She has a stack of fashion magazines with her, fuchsia Post-it notes sticking out. In class, she reads the magazines under her desk. I can tell because the rectangular lights above us reflect off the glossy pages. Brown leather skirts, knee-length knitted socks, turtlenecks in three colors: dark green, lilac, and salt. She says she already started planning her quinceañera, that she has a whole drawer at home full of scraps from magazines, shiny, jagged things, and folded squares of fabric. She says her tía is a seamstress and that sometimes she sends her yellow manila envelopes full of fabric samples. At recess, she shows me pictures. Big poofy dresses with bottoms like gigantic bells. She asks me if I have started planning my quinceañera, and when I say no, I flush with worry—should I have? I do not think mama had a quinceañera.

"Interesting," she says disapprovingly.

Something I do not like about Ana is how she talks about other people, about the "horrible" striped shirt someone wore on a free-dress day when I thought it looked just fine, or if someone's shoes had laces instead of straps, the way some people's backpacks were too bright or too "childish" with action figures, or if they were too plain. "Interesting," she always says. Besides right now, she has never said anything like that about me before, but sometimes I look down at my own backpack and tuck it closer to me.

"Oh," she says. "I almost forgot to tell you! I decided something. I'm going to tell Antonio tomorrow. On the field trip."

My smile falls, and I have to tell my lips to raise it back up. "Tell him what?"

"You know what," she says.

"And he even cut up the strawberries into hearts," I tell mama after school.

Mama looks up from the kitchen counter, a pile of wet potato peels glistening on the wooden cutting board. "That's nice."

"Baba would never have done that," Rafa says.

She sets the peeler down. "That's not true."

I try and remember the little things I learned about Roberto yesterday, to collect them and hold them like tiny diamonds—things like he prefers peppermint to spearmint, that he is allergic to all mangoes except the ones from back home, and that it was a carnation, not a rose, that his mom smashed with the heel of her chancla when she found out he wanted to give it to a girl he liked at school. He was in the tenth grade. His mustache was just starting to fill in, he told me and Ana at dinner last night. "I hated that thing," Ana's mom said, pointing to his lips. "Scratchy."

If I remember these things, maybe he will call me "mija" again. "Mija, how did you remember all that?" he will say, leaning over, impressed. Mama, the security guard at the bank, and abuelo—they all call me "mija," I know, but it is different. Part of me wishes they would say it less often so the word does not wear out, the way fabric loses its color in the sun.

For now, I try to remember: peppermint-not-spearmint, only-mangoes-from-home, carnation-not-rose.

After mama finishes frying strips of lemon pepper chicken for dinner, she signs the permission slip for the field trip tomorrow, a curly blue squiggle at the bottom of the page.

When mama drops us off at school the next morning, she hands me a bagged lunch, the top rolled over itself like fingers tucked into a fist.

"Have fun!" she says, adjusting her mirror before driving off. "Be safe."

I open the bag and glance inside: a peanut-butter-and-jelly sandwich, a bag of potato chips, and an apple sliced the way I like, paper-thin.

Ana waves me over. She called last night to say she had been working on a playlist all week. "Real songs," she said. "The ones my cousin listens to." She wants us to sit in the last row of the bus. "Otherwise I get carsick."

The zoo is half an hour away without traffic, Ms. Walter, the seventh-grade teacher, tells us now. "And up to an hour with traffic. There's always traffic, though," she says, clicking her pen closed. Ms. Clyde stands next to her, rearranging the bandages and wipes in a first aid kit before snapping it shut.

After the teachers take roll, crossing names off a roster attached to a clipboard, they sort us into the two buses. People with last names from *A* through *M* in this bus, by the gate, and *N* through *Z* in that one, by the teacher parking lot. Ana's face falls, the earbud cord dangling from her hands like tangled white thread. We are in separate buses.

"It's okay," I tell her. "I'll see you there, okay?"

Then her eyes shift to something behind me, widening, and before I could turn around, someone pulls my elbow back. A rush of cinnamon. Nutmeg. A wooded forest. I look up. Antonio.

"What do you want?" Ana says, shoving the earbuds into her pocket. I know she likes him, but when she talks to him like this I wonder how much she means it.

"I have to ask you something," he says, looking at me. "In private." Ana frowns at him, or me, I am not sure. Antonio pulls at my elbow again, and the spot where he touches me comes alive with its own heartbeat, its own warmth and mind. He motions toward the line forming at the entrance of the bus.

"Want the front or back?"

"Of what?" I ask.

"The bus. We're sitting together," he says. "I decided."

I look at the bus. "Front," I say, or try to, but it comes out all quiet. I clear my throat. "Front."

Ms. Clyde, tapping her clipboard with her pencil, calls Ana over. "Honey, we don't have all day," she says.

Ana grunts, grabs her lunch box from the ground, and walks toward the gate. She looks back at us before she boards the bus.

"Seat belts, everyone, please and thank you," the bus driver says, turning to face us as we walk in. He is wearing a vest with a single red button in the middle, a lanyard around his neck jingling with shiny gold keys.

Antonio lets me take the window seat. The seats are scratched up and bursting apart, yellow foam poking out around the sides. The seat belts black snakes with metal faces. When I grab mine, Antonio reaches over my lap to put it on for me. I hold my breath. The seat belt clicks, metal into metal.

"Thank you," I say.

A minute later, when we are all buckled in, Father Charles steps into the bus wearing sunglasses. He asks us to quiet down, pushing the glasses up to the top of his head.

I lean over to Antonio. "Is he coming with us?"

"I don't think so," he says. "That would be weird."

"Good morning, everyone. Just wanted to say a blessing for your field trip today, if you could all join me in prayer," he says, closing his eyes and pressing his palms together. After he finishes, I keep my head down so he will not see me.

When he leaves, I notice that I am one, maybe two centimeters away from Antonio. I see the hair raising on my arm and wish

I had shaved, even though mama would not have let me. Our shirts are about to touch. I look down—our shirts are touching.

"How's your mom?" he asks, smiling.

I breathe out. "She's good."

"That reminds me, there's something I've been wanting to ask you," he says. I swallow. "Well, actually, something my mom wants me to ask. I know people can be weird about these things, especially if it's a family thing." He clears his throat. "But the pozole recipe. Do you think your mom could send it?"

I smile, feeling the pang of disappointment, the lightness of relief. "I'll ask."

The bus shifts forward, pulling us with it. He scoots closer. Our knees touch. I turn away from him.

"It's freezing in here," a seventh-grade girl a few rows behind us says, rubbing her arms.

Antonio takes off his jacket and throws it across the bus to her. "Thank you," she says. She and her friend giggle.

He points things out to me as we drive by them, the department store where his dad works the evening shift as a security guard, the perfume shop that his sisters—he has so many of them, he calls them a "swarm," a swarm of sisters—visit before going on dates, using up all the tester bottles. We pass the shoe store with an inflatable sneaker attached to the roof, the parks, a flock of pigeons flying away from the park benches, lifting off into the sky like a hundred gray balloons.

"You tired?" he says. "You can sleep on my shoulder if you want."

"I'm not tired."

"Come here," he says, pulling me to him.

The girls behind us aww and ooh.

“Stop,” I say, and lift myself off him, then turn to face the window, red. After a few minutes, he goes to sit with the boys in the back of the bus.

When we arrive at the zoo, Ms. Clyde hands each of us a ticket to scan at the entrance. I scan mine and push through the revolving door and find Ana.

“I had to sit next to Ashley,” Ana says, like it is my fault. She crosses her arms. “Ashley, of all people.”

“I’m sorry.”

“Oh, right, I forgot. You two are best friends now.”

“Not best friends.”

“Right.” She clears her throat. “And Antonio? Where is he?”

“Not sure,” I say, then point to Ms. Clyde. “Oh, look, I think she’s calling us.”

After roll call, Ms. Clyde hands each of us a bingo sheet. The sixth graders are supposed to identify different ecosystems and the animals that belong in each one, crossing them off the sheet as we go along. The seventh graders, who are starting their genetics unit, are supposed to make note of “phenotypic variety within species.” When we find Antonio, Ana asks him what that means. He says he has no idea.

“Does everyone have a pen?” Ms. Clyde asks, holding a bunch of them in her hand.

In the aquatic section we watch seals slip into the water, fizzy where they darted in, like carbonation bubbles. There are hammerheads with leather-rough skin, silver moonfish with yellow fins, a tank full of gray fish who seem to share one mind, flinching together, turning left at the same time. If only I had my old camera. It is at the house. In my drawer. If I had it, I would take pictures of all the exhibits and then print them out to paint at home. I know Ana brought hers. It is hanging off her wrist, attached by a strap.

"Can I borrow this?"

"Sure." She hands it to me, shows me how to use it. I snap a picture of the jellyfish tank, lit up by a purple backlight.

"Thanks."

On our way to the rainforest section, we pass the food carts with wet hot dogs spinning on a roller grill, popcorn heaped into buckets with rope handles. We pass pink clouds of cotton candy, scoops of ice cream speckled with toppings: blueberries, sprinkles, marshmallows in the shapes of zoo animals.

While Ana uses the bathroom, I stop in front of an eagle whose enclosure is so small, it cannot even stretch out its wings all the way.

"Real beauty, huh?" a tall man in a hat says to me.

I nod, then look back at the eagle, who is ruffling its feathers, using its beak to scratch at its black belly. The man is holding something shiny out in the palm of his hand. A quarter. "Looks even better in real life." Then he hands it to me. "Want it? It's a collector's edition."

Ms. Clyde comes and puts her hands on my shoulders, pulling me away from him. "You really shouldn't approach children like that," she tells him.

I look at the man, who looks at Ms. Clyde. "Oh, I didn't mean anything by it, miss," he says, embarrassed. He puts his hands in his pockets and pulls out a badge, a panda sticker in the bottom corner. "I work here."

When he leaves, Ms. Clyde turns to me. "You need to be more careful than that."

"I didn't do anything. I'm just waiting for Ana." I turn away from her and start walking toward the bathroom before she can say anything else.

"Sofia," she says. "Don't walk away from me when I'm talking to you."

I open the bathroom door and find Ana by the mirrors fixing her hair. The door closes behind me, swinging until it stops. I wash my hands.

After lunch, with our bingo sheets completed, Ana tells me and Antonio she has one more thing she wants to see before we leave. We are standing in front of a herd of giraffes as tall as construction cranes, watching as they bend down to eat from green buckets. "The flamingos," she says, but Antonio does not hear. He is distracted by a man selling cookies, the students around us digging into their pockets and then waving dollar bills in the air like leaves.

"Do you want one?" Antonio asks me.

"She never does," Ana says, then tugs at his arm. "But the flamingos—"

Antonio takes a couple of dollar bills out from his wallet, looks over at me, and smiles. "Two, please," he says to the man. He hands the cookie to me in a napkin. Warm, the chocolate melting. Antonio's hand stays there, above mine for a second, just a second too long. Ana sees it, I know she does.

She yanks the cookie out of my hands, then throws it to the ground, like a character in a soap opera.

"What's your problem?" she says to me. When she walks off, Antonio follows her.

I stare at the cookie. A second later Ms. Clyde comes by, points to it, and tells me not to litter. I pick it up and throw it away.

Some weekends, when it is warm enough, we swim in Ana's pool, throwing her old Barbies to the bottom, their hair in messy knots, then diving down to save them. Whether Ana likes me or not depends on Antonio—if he waves to me at school, the whole day is soured. But mama and Ana's parents get along ever since the three of them met at a parent volunteer event. The twins, entranced by Rafa, follow him around everywhere he goes.

The aquamarine ripples reach me every time Rafa cannonballs into the deep end, plugging his nose. We come out of the pool to eat handfuls of tortilla chips, dipping them into a small red bowl of pico de gallo, lemon-wet cilantro leaves and diced onions and tomatoes in the cupped palm of each chip. Other times, we go out: to the movies, a museum, the park. One time, Ana asked her parents if she could invite Antonio, but they said no. With Rafa as the exception, her parents do not want her to be around boys anymore, now that we are At That Age. Especially not ones older than her.

"It's just by a year. He's our friend," she said. "Right, Sofia?"

"Yes. Right."

And still, they said no.

Mama acts all motherly around Ana's mom. She does things she would not normally do if it was just me and her, like insisting she hold my hand when we cross the street. Or telling me to hold still so she can redo my ponytail. Or pressing a hand into my back so I stand straighter. The way she talks to me only in Spanish around her—"Ven, mija," she says, patting the spot next to her with her palm—annoys me, like it is a show and she keeps nudging me with the script.

"Careful," she says to me now, handing me a plastic butter knife to cut a meatball in half at Mia and Olivia's birthday party. "Remember how to use it?"

"What, the knife? Of course I know how to use it," I say, looking at her. It infuriates me how she acts like I do not know things. She reaches for my hair, but I pull away. Around us, children chase children, ice cream dribbling down their wrists. "Sofia doesn't let me play with her hair anymore," she tells Ana's mom. "Or hug her."

"I just don't like it," I say, embarrassed.

"So moody, aren't they, at this age?" Mama looks over at the other moms, who nod, twirling spaghetti around plastic forks, drinking soda from cans.

And it stings. "I'm not moody."

Mama laughs and then looks at the other moms, as if saying, See? Juana puts her hands up like, What are we supposed to do?

"I'm not, though," I say, looking at them, the moms. They laugh again.

"It's okay, honey. We all go through that phase," Juana says, touching my shoulder.

Mama pulls me back to her, tells me I have a knot in my hair and to sit still as she unties it. I do not want to be called moody again so I stay there, even though it feels like chest pain, bright and pulsing, what I want to say.

I push myself free.

“Come here,” she says, pulling me back. “Sit still. Your hair’s all tangled.”

“No thanks,” I say, walk toward the pool, and jump in.

"Should I get this?" mama asks me a few days later, holding up a bottle of wine. We are at the grocery store picking up some snacks for later tonight, board game night with Ana's family. Rafa has already called dibs on the thimble for Monopoly.

"Sure," I say. "I think I remember Ana saying her mom likes wine."

Mama laughs. "Oh, Juana definitely likes wine."

She places the bottle in the shopping cart and pushes it forward, past the free sample stands and toward the express checkout line. When she pulls out her debit card to pay, I hold my breath, waiting until Pending turns to Approved, until the small green arrow flashes on the screen, to let it out. Last week, it said Declined when she tried to pay for laundry detergent, and mama, with a face as red as the *X* on the screen, told the cashier she would have to come back later to buy it, apologizing quietly as she put her card back into her wallet.

"What about the forty that abuelo gave you for Christmas?" I asked her in line.

She looked up at the cashier again. "Sorry about that," she said, ignoring me.

"And mine? My forty?" I asked her in the car. "Can I have it?"

"Later," she said, gripping the steering wheel.

But now it is green, and the machine is printing out a receipt. A long scroll of coupons at the bottom we can clip when we get home.

It is Sunday. Mama is at work and Rafa is fast asleep on the couch, sleepy from the warm sun leaking into the living room through the cracked kitchen window, the cushions littered with dinosaurs, like the aftermath of a meteor, their bodies scattered, sideways, bent, when the doorbell rings. I have just finished painting the jellyfish from the zoo on a sheet of printer paper. I twist the cap onto the last paint tube, rinse the brushes in the cup of water, wipe my hands on my jeans, and walk toward the door.

My fingers hovering above the doorknob, I think about what people say about opening the door for strangers and almost decide not to. But then I catch a glimpse of him through the window. The sleeve of his gray striped shirt.

"Nina, I know you're in there," I hear him shout. "You, too, Sofia. Rafael." I turn toward Rafa. I have the urge to cover his ears with my hands like earmuffs, to let him sleep.

"Rafa," I say, walking over to him, tapping him on the collarbone until he wakes up. I whisper, unsure if baba can hear me through the door. "Go nap in our room."

He wakes up alarmed, eyes wide.

"Shh, it's okay," I tell him. "Just go to our room."

When I hear our bedroom door close, I walk toward the front

door again. I hear everyone say it in my mind. "Don't open the door for anyone when I'm not home," says mama. "Don't do it," says abuelo. "Don't you dare." But something tugs at me, and there are my fingers now, touching the bruised metal of the door knob.

"It's not mine, I—" baba starts. "Oh. Sofia, hi," he says when he sees me. He has a beard now, hair sprouting thick along his jawline and above his chin and upper lip in dark patches. Besides that, he looks the same. Same medium frame, same focused look ahead. For some reason, I thought he would look different. Maybe part of me wants him to. I try to locate the grief on his body—where our loss has plumped him up or thinned him out—but I cannot find it.

"What isn't yours?" I ask.

"Where's your mom?"

"She isn't here right now."

"She left you two here alone? What a god-awful mom, I tell you—"

And it is simple. I do not think about it. I close the door.

But he pounds on it. Hard, so hard that I think he must be throwing his entire body against the door, so loud that Rafa is surely awake by now, pulling the sheets over himself to hide or crouching down under the bed for cover. I imagine him scared, shaking, and widen my stance. I press my hands against the door with all of my strength. I slide the door chain into the latch. "Sofia, come on," baba says. "Let me in."

"Stop, please," I whisper, embarrassed about how much noise he is making. I almost let him in just for it to be quiet again. I back away and stare at the lock, waiting for it to snap off. After a few minutes, or maybe just a few seconds, I hear what sounds like a whole key ring of keys jingling, the heavy thuds of footsteps.

"Sir, step back, please," I hear a deep voice say, followed by a blip, then static.

"No, it's okay. My kids live here."

"Does he live here?" the deep voice asks.

"No," says a familiar voice. Lucas.

"Never seen him before," says someone else. Our neighbor, Arthur. "That's why I called."

"I swear, man, my kids are in there. Sofia. Come on."

A few seconds later: "Sofia!"

"Listen," says Lucas, pulling me aside after. "We don't like this here, all this drama. Really ticks off the manager. Between you and me, she's kicked people out for much less. Try not to let this happen again, okay?"

Later, when the shelter writes up their report, it says that one of their residents complained to the local police department about a "suspicious-looking person" upstairs, attempting "forced entry." "Accosting" the people in Unit 29. I had to look up that word, typing it into the search bar on the computer the next time I went to the library. They asked him to "leave the premises." He agreed. No charges. Sealed, filed. "Archived."

When Lucas and the officer leave, I put my back to the door and cry, finally cry, unplugging the drain and letting it gush out. My neck is wet. I stare at the floor and the tiles are blurry. My head, a heavy, unbalanced stone on my body. My eyes hurt. Rafa comes out of our room thirty minutes later and sits down next to me. He looks confused.

"You slept through that?" I ask, taking the wad of tissue he hands me, blowing my nose.

"Through what?"

When I tell mama, I am surprised she is not angry with me for opening the door. Mostly she is upset that I did not call her when it happened. "You're supposed to tell me these things, Sofia," she says, shaking her head. "Oh—oh no, hey, what's wrong?"

"I let them think I didn't know him," I say, rubbing my eyes, feeling it about to start again. I try and swallow it down, but it finds its way out, a hiccup caught in my throat. It leaks through my eyes, my nose. I want to pull my hoodie over my head. I want it to be dark, and I want to be alone, but mama brings me close to her chest. My cheek is pressed against the chain of her necklace.

"Shh," she says, rubbing my back in long strokes. "It's okay. You're okay. Rafa's okay. Even stupid baba is okay, all right?"

When I hear a knock on the bathroom door, I jump back. But it is only Rafa. How much he looks like baba here, in this light, walking through the door. He bends down, holding a glass of water. They have the same hands.

"Thank you," mama says. She takes the glass and gives it to me. "Drink," she says. "It's okay."

A few weeks later, Rafa walks up to mama, who is sitting at the dining table rubbing her forehead, and hands her a stack of printer paper. "I don't get it. Roberto can have all of my paper," he says.

"It's a different type of paper," mama says.

Rafa looks up at her. "Oh," he says. "Lined?"

"No, honey."

Juana had just called. Mama did a lot of soothing, saying, "Don't worry, oh, don't worry, it will be fine," and it was comforting, seeing mama be a mama to another mama. She told her she would help, and I wondered what she meant by that, what she can actually do. Juana said a problem with Roberto's papers have held him up at the border, that he went to Mexico to attend his mom's funeral last week and now they are not sure when he will be allowed back into the country. I ask her if Ana is okay.

"She's worried, of course. I mean, why wouldn't she be?" she says. "Juana says she'll be absent tomorrow. Maybe you can keep track of her schoolwork for her. I think that would be a nice thing to do." Mama says she has sent them flowers. Violets.

Juana's favorite. Earlier today, she went to the grocery store to buy ingredients to make them all dinner for the week. I take the receipt from the bag. "Isn't this expensive?" I ask. I look down at my shoes, which have begun to tear at the front, the soles on each shoe hanging like a floppy rubber tongue. What she spent on groceries would have been enough to buy me at least two more pairs. Actually, this reminds me I want to show her a pair I found in a magazine ad, white sneakers with a small gold heart stitched into the sides. I will ask her later.

"So," I say, looking down at the table. "What does this mean?"

Mama leans back in her chair. "They don't know yet. It's probably just a mistake."

"I mean, is he a citizen?"

"I don't know, Sofia. I didn't ask."

I play with my hands, tying the straw wrapper Rafa left on the kitchen counter into a loose knot, then untying it. I feel my eyes well up, but mama is watching me, so I blink fast and hope my eyes are not too glassy. I know if I started to cry, she would tell me Roberto is not my dad, not even close. She would say it to try and make me feel better, I know, taking my hands in hers, telling me I do not know him *that* well. But I think that would make me cry more. So for now, I am focusing on blinking, not thinking about the lunch bag or the strawberry hearts, not hearing the gentleness when he calls me "mija," which not even baba has called me before. I stand up and excuse myself, walking to the bathroom. I lean against the sink. I turn on the faucet all the way so no one can hear me cry, and even then, it is like the water is telling me to "shh."

After a few minutes, someone knocks on the door. For a brief second, I think it is baba there, knocking, and what he must think of me crying over a different dad. "All good in there?" she says.

I shut off the faucet. I dry my face on a towel. "All good."

Ana misses school for the first week of February. Juana says Ana refuses to get out of bed, that all she will eat are crackers, and even then, only a few at a time, or else it all comes back up. Roberto is still not home.

"I had to put a trash can by her bed. And cleaning spray," she tells mama over the phone.

I imagine Ana all alone in her room, staring at the picture of her family she keeps on her desk. Maybe she uses tally marks in her journal to keep track of how long he has been gone.

I want to try and help, but mama says sometimes the best way to help someone is to give them space. Whenever mama gets off the phone with Juana, I tell her to say hi to Ana for me, and that I have an extra set of notes for her from school. Mama says that Juana says that Ana says thank you, and this is how we talk now—with "Tell her" and "She says" and "Make sure that she knows." She just does not feel like talking to anyone, not even to her sisters, Juana explains.

Antonio says that everyone at school knows what happened and that he is sure Ana will never come back.

"Why not?" I ask him.

"She's embarrassed," he says. "Imagine if everyone at school knew that you live in a homeless shelter. You'd probably be too embarrassed to show your face here again."

I look down. "She probably just misses her dad."

Later that day, Ms. Clyde addresses the topic in class. "I have some sad news to share," she says. "I take it, by now, you've noticed one of your peers has not been in class these past few days. It's a sad situation, really. Anyway, I wanted to bring this up so we can keep Ana and her family in our prayers. Sofia, why don't you lead today's prayer? A Prayer for Immigrants? It's on page one thirty-seven of the prayer book, if you want to read from there. Or you can speak from your heart." She walks toward my desk, handing me the prayer book, a green tab sticking out.

But I do not take it from her. I let her hold it in the air, above my desk, thinking about how Ana would do the same if she were here. With each passing second, I feel more eyes on me, see more of my classmates turning around to face me. My hands are shaking. I fold them underneath my desk.

"Sofia," Ms. Clyde says, setting the book on my desk. She taps on it with her long red nails. There is a silver sequin glued onto each one. "Earth to Sofia."

"No thank you," I say, quiet but firm. I look up at her. By now the entire class has turned around. Even the betta fish, with its magenta body resting on a plastic leaf, looks up.

"I'm not asking, Sofia. Page one-three-seven."

I shake my head.

"Sofia!" she says, exasperated, her hands on her hips.

I look up and from the corner of my eye, I see Ashley raise her hand. "I can do it," she says.

"I didn't call on you, Ashley," Ms. Clyde says.

"But I really want to," Ashley says. "I think," she says, pausing, "well, I think God wants me to. It's hard to explain, but—"

"All right, all right," says Ms. Clyde, straightening out her shirt before turning around.

I mouth "thank you" to Ashley, who nods at me and stands up to take the book from Ms. Clyde. She flips it open and begins to read.

During lunch, Antonio insists we act like things are normal.

"But they're not," I say.

"Well, we can act like they are."

I frown at how childish he sounds. Crossing his arms like this, he reminds me of Rafa except whinier. I look at him and it is as if I see Rafa's face on Antonio's body. It catches me off guard how quickly what I had been storing up until now—the warmth, the sweetness toward him—starts to dissolve into the air around me, like an exhale.

I take a bite out of my sandwich. "Why would we do that?"

"Because, I told you, people like us—"

"Have to stay together, right." It comes out more annoyed than I would have liked it to. I dab the edge of my mouth with a napkin.

Lately, Antonio has stopped playing four square with the older kids. He does not even wave as he passes them on the way to class, like he usually does. Instead, these past few days, he sits with me. Sometimes we work on homework together, and other times, we talk—about Ana, about his dad, about mine. When I try to switch the conversation to Spanish, he stops me.

"What is it?" I ask him.

"What is what?"

"Why can't I speak Spanish?" I say, and when he does not respond, I add, "Since when do you listen to the vice principal?"

"Can you stop?" he says. He peels open his yogurt, dipping his spoon inside to mix it. Even the way he does this is forceful. Angry. Some yogurt splatters on the table in a wet glop. When baba would get like this, we waited quietly for it to pass, for him to collect himself again. I do the same now, studying the folds of my napkin.

"The other kids just don't get it," he says, calmer now. "They call me things. And I can handle it. I just don't want them to start calling you things too. Or Ana, if she ever comes back."

"She will come back," I say. Then a second later, "What kind of things?"

He mixes his yogurt. We eat the rest of our lunch in silence. No Spanish. No English.

When Ana returns to school, she walks toward the kindergarten classroom after hugging her mom goodbye, holding Olivia's hand in one hand and Mia's hand in the other. I run up to her. She tells her sisters to head inside, to hurry so they will not be late.

"Sofia," she says, and her eyes are puffy and red and swollen. She starts off okay but then catches and misses her breath, choking on it, one hand rising to cover her mouth. "My mom said it could be a while before he comes back."

I hug her. "I know, I'm so sorry," I tell her.

"And Ms. Clyde kept calling my house phone, telling me I needed to send in my homework."

"I have some more notes and assignments in my folder to give you," I say, patting my backpack.

"And they said because of all the school I missed, that I might need to repeat sixth grade. And then you and I won't be in the same class and my mom would need to pay for another year of tuition and now she can't because my dad isn't here to help."

"Hey," I tell her. "We'll figure it out, okay?"

She blows her nose into her tissue. "Okay," she says.

Ana walks to the bathroom to splash her face with cold water.

I take Olivia's lunch box, which she forgot to give her, and knock on the kindergarten classroom's door to hand it to the teacher. I tell Ana the same thing mama told her mom, "No te preocupes"—in Spanish so she knows that I mean it. By lunch, she is imitating John-Isaac from our class, laughing over and over at the way he says "cantaloupe," forgetting about it and then remembering and laughing about it all over again throughout the day, and I want to believe mama, that everything will be fine.

When it seems safe to do so, I ask about her dad. Where in Mexico was he? What was he doing there to pass the time? She says he has been at his cousin's house. On the phone, on hold with some agency most of the time. I picture him with a phone pressed to his ear, leaning against the wall, then pacing around the room in circles. Peppermint-not-spearmint, only-mangoes-from-home, carnation-not-rose.

"Has he asked about school?"

"Every time he calls," she says.

I want her to say he asks about me too. About how I am doing in school. How mama and Rafa are doing. But she does not bring it up.

"Has he asked about me?" I finally say.

She zips up her lunch box. "Why would he?" she asks, unfolding her napkin.

I shrug, embarrassed. "I don't know." I scoot my chair in, thinking about the car ride, the neon, and here it is: the border of his care, the edge of it. I try to change the subject, looking at the gray slice of sky out the cafeteria window. "It's going to rain all day, isn't it?"

"How would I know?" she says. "Why'd you have to bring him up?" she asks, her bottom lip trembling. "I don't want to talk about it."

"I'm sorry," I say, and watch as she puts her thermos in her lunch box, her water bottle, her spoon. "Ana." She moves to another table alone.

I sigh, staring at the reflection of myself in the laminated surface of the wood. I lift my backpack onto the bench of the cafeteria table and pull out my lunch box. Mama microwaved frozen chicken tenders with pale breadcrumbs this morning, and here, in this lighting, they look like they were dipped, or maybe dropped, in sand. I double-check my math homework, skimming my pencil over the numbers. Outside, the sky is like gray and white paint swirled together. It keeps us all inside for recess.

It happens after Rafa asks mama for an action figure he saw in a store window, half man, half wolf, arm bent into a punch: she tells him no. The sale sticker is on the bottom right corner of the box. A bright red circle, like someone stuck a pepperoni on it. Fifteen percent off.

"But it's not even full price," Rafa says, whining. He tugs on her jacket. A woman passes by us, pushing a stroller. A small brown dog trots behind her, wagging its tail.

Mama keeps walking. "For your birthday."

"Am I even getting birthday presents this year?" Rafa says, the skin around his nose wrinkling. "Am I having a birthday party?"

I look over at her, at her face, which looks like it is caught in something, a bug in a web. I think about what I will ask for this year: a twenty-four set of gel pens, twelve with glitter, twelve without. Or scented markers. Or a pair of skates. A new camera. But mostly, I need new shoes.

"We have this conversation every five minutes, Rafa."

"Okay, fine," he says, and I look over at him, surprised that he dropped it that easily. Mama relaxes for a second. "Then can we get my toys from the house? I can call baba. I can do it right now," he says, reaching into mama's purse for her phone.

"God, Rafa, can you just—"

"I can get my magazines from my room," I say, thinking of the one with the otter on the cover, with an article about seahorses. It had a zoomed-in picture of seahorse babies, as small as fingernail clippings. "And my camera."

"No," mama says, like it was obvious.

"Then I hate you," Rafa says. It is the way he says it. Flat. Matter-of-fact. Not icy or hot but room temperature, like it is something he has considered for a long time, like it is something he learned about in school.

Mama looks at the ground. It seems like she is holding her breath, looking at the sidewalk, and I cannot see her eyes. "Watch him," she says, then walks inside the toy store.

He says nothing at first.

"You don't feel bad about what you said?"

"I want my toys," he says.

"They're just toys."

Then the chime of the bell on the door. When mama comes back, she hands him the action figure. He squeals. Giggly, bouncy, swinging the bag in his hands forward, then back. He asks what is for dinner, and mama looks ahead, shaking her head.

"Can I get something too?" I ask.

She does not respond.

I feel it rising in me, a tide. A swell in my chest. I speak without thinking. "I don't get it. You got Rafa something, a stupid toy, but I don't get anything? I need new shoes. I mean, look at them." When she looks at my shoes, which look fine from up here, just a little scratched, I feel embarrassed. I want to take them off to show her the soles, the way they flop out, but she is already walking toward the car.

Fuming, she drives me to a shoe store.

"Five minutes," she says.

I pick out a pair with a blue stripe.

When her credit card declines, she rummages inside her bag for another one.

"Thank you," I say, holding the box after.

"What's for dinner?" Rafa asks.

"Just stop," she says quietly. "Please."

A knock at the door.

Seven a.m., Saturday, and mama is still sleeping.

"Come in," I say after I look through the peephole, and he does come in. Lucas hands me a paper, turns it face down, and says he likes the chili plant we have outside. I say he can grab a pepper off the stem if he likes.

"Give this to your mom. Tell her to see me if she has any questions. Otherwise, it's by noon tomorrow," he says, and closes the door behind him.

I flip the paper over, then read the first sentence. I fold it back up.

Eight a.m. now and mama is awake. She stretches upward as she walks into the living room, pajamas wrinkled with sleep, hair in messy yarn-like stretches across her chest. I fold the paper into a square. Yawning, she offers me coffee.

"I'll be right back," I say.

I walk outside, down the metal stairs, then rush back inside, running to get the white envelope from inside my pillowcase. It is still there, right where I put it. Then I reach into my backpack and grab a paper from my folder. When I get to the main lobby, I push open the heavy glass door and ask Lucas where the manager is. He says she is not here. I say that I saw her car parked outside and that it is not lunchtime, so she cannot be on her lunch break, and then she walks into the room holding a pen.

"Are you the manager?" I ask.

She nods. "Can I help you?"

"I'd like to talk to you." I feel myself trembling a little. I hope that me trembling is like the wrinkles on my school uniform, that you can really only tell from up close.

"Ruth," Lucas says. "She's one of the kids from Unit Twenty-Nine. I just gave her the notice."

"Oh," she says. She looks sympathetic, tilts her head to the side. "Honey."

"I want to talk with you in your office," I say. "Now, please."

She hesitates, nods, then gestures to the hallway. "Go ahead."

When we get to her office, she pulls out a red chair for me and tells me to sit down. "I know why you're here," she says. "It's really not in our control. It's a matter of policy. Your mother's check bounced." She thumbs through a file on her desk.

"For how much?" I ask. I look down at my shoes, at the blue stripe on each one.

She shifts in her seat and straightens out her dress. "This isn't really something we discuss with, uh," she says, searching for a word, "you know, kids." She reaches into a drawer and hands me a brochure. "We have all of our policies here in case your mother wants to read it. We have a Spanish version, too, if she needs it."

"My mom speaks fluent English."

She puts a hand up. "Let me finish. There really isn't anything we can do. Now, if you'll just please," she says, pointing at the door, then looking down at her watch. "I'm supposed to be on a call right now."

"Hold on," I say, standing up so I can reach into my pocket. I pause, my hand on the envelope, wondering if I am about to make a mistake, but I do not know what else to do. I pinch my lips together, take out the white envelope, then slide it onto her desk between her keyboard and the long white cord of her mouse. She takes it.

"I'm sorry, but," she says, pausing. Then she laughs. "Are you trying to bribe me? I don't think you want to try and bribe me, sweetheart."

"I'm not trying to bribe you." I take the envelope back, open it, and hand her the cash. "It's for the rent."

She hesitates, then counts it. "That's not enough."

I swallow. "How much more, then?"

The phone rings, a small red light flashing on the base of the landline. "I have to take this." She reaches for the phone. I place my hand on top of it.

"Please," I say. "How much more?"

"It's too late." She pulls the phone out from underneath my hand. "A new family is moving in next week. And this," she says, pointing to the space between us, to the phone. "We don't do this here. This is inappropriate. I'll be discussing this with your mother."

I point to the cash. "Then I'll take that back."

She shakes her head, slips the money beneath the corner of her mouse pad. "Your mother still owes the money," she says. "I'm going to hold on to this." Then she picks up the phone and puts her hand over the receiver. The light flashes, green now, and she opens the drawer, pulling out a pen. "You need to go now, okay? I can't do anything for you."

As fast as I can, I lift the mouse pad, grab the cash, and run out of the office despite the "Hey" and then "Hey!" from the housing manager and the "Come back here!" that she yells, calling out from the doorframe, and I am running, running up the stairs and through the front door of our unit, and there is mama in the kitchen stirring beans on the stove, flipping tortillas on a bare flame. I bend over, catching my breath. She looks up every few seconds to follow the news on the TV, the volume loud and rumbling in our small apartment. She scrapes the bottom of the pot, metal against metal, singing to herself. She clanks the spoon against the pot loudly until the beans slide off. Rafa is awake, too, now, tapping his pencil against the spiral of his notebook, kicking his leg against the foot of the couch. The weather forecaster makes a joke. The other weather forecaster fake laughs.

Mama asks where I went, and I say for a walk, and she says I never answered her about the coffee so she just made me a cup anyway. I take the warm mug from her hands. "Thank you."

"You know, we never celebrated Thanksgiving. I bought a turkey we could make later. But I guess I should start defrosting it now, shouldn't I?" She looks at the watch on her wrist.

I shake my head. "Mama."

"What? It's not that big. Shouldn't take that long. You can invite Ana and . . ." She pauses. "What's his name?"

"Antonio."

"Right, Antonio." She motions to my hands with her chin. "And what's that?"

I look down at my report card. "Oh," I say. "Nothing." I was going to show the manager my grades. Straight A's. It was meant to be proof—that we are the good kind.

She turns around, bends down to the freezer, and takes out the turkey, a large white-and-blue bag with yellow netting. She plops it in the sink, full of water.

I shake my head. "Wait, mama."

"Hm?"

I hand her the eviction notice.

"Oh," she says. Just that. She looks at the turkey in the sink. It bobs up in the water. Her hand falls to her side, holding the note.

"I tried," I say, looking down at my shoes. "To get them to let us stay, I mean."

When the housing manager walks up the stairs with Lucas and a security guard, mama turns to me. "What did you do?"

We drive.

(past blue houses, through dark narrow tunnels, on the highway that slopes over the hill, past a hospital—*I used to work there, you know*—past a shut-down amusement park, the entrance crisscrossed with caution tape, to school and back, to drop-off at seven, to the clinic after school, past a lipstick factory spewing pink smoke, past beach towels drying on clotheslines, toward the cemetery, to abuela—*Do you want to say hello? Pick some flowers to bring her?*—past the community garden, past the zucchini plot, the pomegranate tree bent like an old lady, to the library, past the windmills waving goodbye, on the dirt road behind the smoothie place, past a church with a marble staircase, on the freeway at seventy-five miles an hour, past a state line, then back a state line)

We park.

(under mango trees, by the coffee shop, in dust, in dusk, in silver puddles, dizzy in a swarm of dragonflies, on a patch of grass by a field of persimmons, by the baseball diamond, in blue lights, in reverse, outside the liquor store, in the gray shade of an oak tree, for a dollar an hour, with quarters, a mile away from a tornado, by the hotel at six forty-five, with the sunroof down, in a dark corner, in secret)

We sleep.

(we try)

For a week.

Mama turns to me on the eighth day.

"I have an idea. What if I taught you how to drive right now? I mean, do you want to? Well, come. Let's switch places. There you go, mija. Seat belt. Adjust your mirrors—yup, that button over there. And your seat. Adjust that too. There should be a lever on the side. Okay. Sit up. Hands like this on the steering wheel—no, like this. The brake is this one. The other one's the gas. Yes. Slowly. Just try. I'm right here. Careful! Slow. Okay, good. Drive to the end of the street. Good, good. Keep going. Almost there and . . . brake. Okay, now keep going. Slow, now. Careful with the speed bump. You did it! At least this one thing I have taught you."

On the ninth day, the day before his birthday, Rafa unfolds a list.

"It doesn't have to be anything big, but here's what I was thinking. Jake had a bouncy castle but that's for babies, I think, so maybe a water slide. Probably hot dogs and s'mores. But Samuel can't have marshmallows so he'll just have the chocolate and graham crackers." He skims lower down his list. "And for presents," he says, flipping over the paper.

I put my hand on his arm. "Please stop."

After we finished packing the day we got the notice, Juana, who said we could stay with her for a few days, called to say she changed her mind and that she was sorry, there was too much going on at home. Through the line I heard Ana's laugh, the giggle of the twins.

"Roberto just got home," said Juana. "The neighbor—you remember Rose—well, she wants to throw a welcome home party for him. Today! I haven't even started on the cake," she said, exasperated. "No, Olivia, give it back. Your sister had it first." Her voice sounded far away. "Anyway."

Mama said she understands and hung up.

Mr. Leonard's place was booked through the first week of July. Ms. Monique asked if we would like to put our name down on a list. We would be number twenty-two—not on the list, the wait list. Mama said all right.

Antonio lives in a two-bedroom house with his mom, dad, swarm of sisters, aunt, and three cousins. "I could ask if we can stay with him," I said, the thought of sleeping in the same space, of us breathing so close to each other, a familiar pang. Faint but still a pang. "Let me call him." I reached for her phone. He did not respond. I left a message. The next day, I called and left a message. I called the day after that and left a message. The day after that, I called and left a message. The day after that—

The priest's voicemail box was full. "Have a blessed day," it said before ending the call in a beep.

"Fuck," mama said.

I rested my head on the seat belt strap, looking out the window at the new leaves shivering on their branches, the blood-orange sky. We could ask abuelo, I thought.

"Mama, we could go to—" But the suggestion felt wrong in my mouth.

"To?"

"Abuelo."

"No," she gasped. Her hand reached for her arm, rubbed it in circles. As if I hit her.

"The gift card," mama says on the thirteenth day. The sunroof is down. The sky above us, bleeding, red clouds clotting in the orange sunset. "I know you wanted to save it, but," she says, looking down at her purse, "I think we're past that now."

I wince, seeing for a second the bright light of the display case. The remaining fifty cents on the card, useless, in my backpack pocket. "I lost it."

"What do you mean, lost it?"

"It must have fallen out of my pocket."

"At school?" she says, placing her hands on the steering wheel like she wants to drive there right now, at seven at night, to look for it, even though Rafa and I have been absent for three days now, since Wednesday, because it was all getting to be too much, mama said, too much. The school is probably closed, locked by now.

"I don't know."

"Just think." She grabs her keys. "Try to remember."

"I said I don't know."

"Oh, you don't know," she says sarcastically, tossing her keys on the floor. "Well, that's perfect."

I close my eyes.

Mama says if your eyelash falls out make a wish so I do—the lashes thin, black parentheses in my palm. I blow them out the window.

A handful of punctuation lands on the asphalt.

"What happened?" she asks in the morning, holding my face between her hands.

I shrug away from her and unfold the mirror. It is more noticeable than I thought, a gap the size of my fingertip in the corner of each eye. I try to fill it in with the other lashes but it does not help. Mama is worried about me, I can tell. But she does not know what I know, that something great will happen today. So many wishes' worth. So I smile wide. All of my teeth. Mama bursts into tears. Takes out her phone. Steps outside. The sun, bright as turmeric. The wishes: iridescent, glowing, expanding. Floating up to the sky like a million bubbles, then popping. The glitter landing on our heads. From far away, it must look like dandruff, I know.

It is seven when he comes. The last of the sunset is fading. A blip of pink there, by the gold clouds. We are parked on a strip of grass by the beach, watching the waves smack the concrete barrier, splashing foam onto the road. Then the tide recedes, apologetic. I see his silhouette first, then him. The sun, a lamp at its lowest setting. Someone unplugs it. He steps into the headlights: arm, leg, face. He is wearing his gray striped shirt. It is bunched up to his elbows.

"Nina," he says, walking up to mama.

Rafa looks up at me, puts his hand on my arm. "What's happening?"

I am too tired to respond.

Has baba grown a fuller beard or is it the night on his face? Mama gets out of the car and runs to him. I put my hands over Rafa's eyes. Baba tells her we will go somewhere together, all four of us. He calls it home. "I'm sorry, okay?" he tells mama, taking both of her hands. "About everything." A glint of moonlight from the face of his wristwatch.

Meanwhile, I look out the window. A star blinks above us like an eye.

He walks toward me and Rafa and opens the door on my side.

I hold my breath. He is about to hug me, then stops. “Habibi,” he says. “What happened to your face?”

A minute later, a blue pickup truck pulls up. The door swings open. When abuelo steps out, baba turns to mama.

“You called your dad?” baba says, and steps back.

“I wasn’t sure if you’d come.”

“I told you I would,” says baba.

Abuelo approaches them. Baba’s shoulders tense, his shirtsleeves tightening around his arms.

I look at the three of them walking toward each other, the ocean thrashing behind them. We cannot hear them anymore. We can only see their hands: baba’s pointing to abuelo, abuelo’s pointing to mama, mama’s holding a wad of tissues, wiping her eyes. We watch until we get drowsy, until the moon falls asleep, too, the clouds covering it like a blanket.

Later, a branch scratches at the window, and I wake up. The moon, uncovered now, turns to face us. Across the street, the three of them are still shouting. But from here, all the way over here, all I can hear are the waves.

ACKNOWLEDGMENTS

Thank you to Ayesha Pande for her unrivaled guidance and expertise. I could not have asked for a better agent, or a more inspiring one. Thank you for all that you do.

Thank you to my editor, Retha Powers, who put so much care into this book. I am deeply grateful for her edits and her vision for the novel, and for everything big and small that she, Leela Gebo, Hannah Campbell, and the rest of the incredible team at Holt did to prepare this book for publication.

Thank you to the MFA program in creative writing at the University of Wisconsin-Madison and the Wisconsin Institute for Creative Writing for introducing me to the kindest, most supportive community of writers I have ever met. To my MFA cohort: Martha Pham, Waringa Hunja, Bella Bravo, and Maddie Curtis; my professors: Beth Nguyen, Dantiel W. Moniz, Porter Shreve, Ron Kuka, and Sean Bishop; my fellowship cohort: Yalitza Ferreras, Steven Espada Dawson, Chessy Normile, and Taymour

Soomro; and my students—thank you. I am more grateful for our time together than I can express. It was perfect, all of it, perfect.

At Stanford University, thank you to the creative writing program and its lecturers, Harriet Clark, Margaret Ross, Keith Ekiss, Brittany Perham, Mark Labowskie, Kate Petersen, Solmaz Sharif, and Shimon Tanaka, for teaching me what I know about writing. I would also like to thank the Major Grant, the Honors in the Arts Program, the QuestBridge Scholars Program, the Leland Scholars Program, and the Milken Scholars Program. Jessi Pipert, thank you for all of your help, even beyond graduation.

At the University of Oxford, thank you to Haydn Middleton for showing me books I would have never found otherwise; I learned so much from you.

Thank you to everyone whose feedback shaped the book—my MFA cohort and professors; my workshop at Tin House led by Zaina Arafat; my workshop at Writers in Paradise led by Luis Alberto Urrea; Jessi Pipert and the Honors in the Arts Program at Stanford University; and Emily Doyle.

I am extremely grateful to Blue Mountain Center, Monson Arts, Kimmel Harding Nelson Center for the Arts, Djerassi, Hedgebrook, Mountain Words, and Ragdale for having me as a writer-in-residence. I am still stunned by the generosity of these residencies and the people who run them; thank you for the time, space, and community. Thank you to Gauri, Esther, Gigi, Kyana, Jessamyn, Laura, Charlie, Okwudili, Anna, Phil, Arvin, Hannah, Brooke, Blanca, Erin, Allyson, Cynthia, Anne, Jason, Layli, Emily, and everyone whose name I missed, for making it all so special. And thank you to the Parkers—Janet, Mark, and Cade—for all of the care packages.

Thank you to the Steinbeck Fellowship, the Martha Heasley

Cox Center for Steinbeck Studies, and Keenan Norris for the generous award.

Emily Doyle—thank you, thank you, thank you. We did it!

Thank you to my mom, brother, and dad. I love you, always.

Thank you to each and every one of my aunts, uncles, and cousins, all of the Rochas, Rizkallas, Castellanos, Kinchlas, Pardues, and Garcias, for their love and support through the years.

Abuela and Teta, thank you for doing so much for me, for giving so much. Abuela, I wish you could have held this book.

Mom, thank you for double-checking my Spanish.

Extra thanks to Yalitza Ferreras, Emily Doyle, Martha Pham, Waringa Hunja, Selby Kia, Emily Wiechman, and Beth Nguyen for all of their behind-the-scenes support. I am so grateful for your friendship.

And finally, Grant. Thank you. You are pure sunlight. You make everything brighter.

ABOUT THE AUTHOR

Amanda Rizkalla is a recent Steinbeck Fellow and Wisconsin Institute for Creative Writing Fellow. She has been a writer-in-residence at Ragdale, Hedgebrook, Djerassi, Mountain Words, the Kimmel Harding Nelson Center for the Arts, Monson Arts, and Blue Mountain Center. After graduating from Stanford University, she received her MFA from the University of Wisconsin–Madison, where she was a Kemper Knapp Fellow. Her work has received support from the Barbara Deming Memorial Fund and has been nominated for the Pushcart Prize.